THE BOXCAR KILLER

M. Hartman

NFB Publishing
Buffalo, New York

NFB
<<<>>>
NFB Publishing/Amelia Press
119 Dorchester Road
Buffalo, New York 14213

For more information visit
Nfbpublishing.com

For Sami

THE BOXCAR KILLER

ONE

I COULD BARELY GET TWO fingers inside my collar as I yanked at the starched material taut against my skin. Balancing on two legs I strained further towards the window maneuvering to the left of the navy blazers that blocked my view of the courtyard. She rounded the path from Rutledge Academy towards Cannon Drive and all heads turned in hypnotic unison. She enveloped us like a warm, lazy fog and right at that very moment, time stood still, and she was forever photographed in my mind. The droning voice at the front of the room faded slowly and then disappeared altogether. Watching her was a complete out of body experience. Her green eyes danced as she threw her head back in laughter. I was consumed by a smile, kind and innocent. The sun illuminated brown and blonde strands of long shiny hair cascaded around a heart shaped face. Her brow creased and her lips full and pink pursed slightly as she studied the page and thoughtfully wrote a final farewell in a Rutledge Academy Class of 1967 Yearbook. Her name was Tessa Rhodes, and she was perfect.

The slam of the book on the desktop was loud. The swish of air and sudden impact knocked me off my chair onto the concrete floor. My papers fluttered about and briefly hung above me like a mobile decorated in numbers, symbols and equations. I hit the ground with a loud thud. The roar of laughter was muffled by the ringing in my head, and I lay there for several minutes unable to breathe let alone get up. Off in the distance I heard a bell clanging and then out of the corner of my eye, a herd of feet and legs eagerly rushing past.

The smell of stale cigar smoke was overwhelming and disgusting. That, as well as my present condition, made me sick to my stomach. He stood over me studying my form with a goofy, perplexed expression. I thought about kicking him in the shins but decided that wasn't the best idea given the fact that I was on the floor.

"Ouch," I mumbled as I carefully lifted myself up and rested my spine against the cold tiled wall. My eyes squinted tight as I cupped the throbbing ache stabbing sharply at the side of my head and felt warm liquid flow from my temple down my cheek.

"That'll teach you," he said pointing his long bony finger down at me.

He had an unconscious habit of spitting when he spoke with any shred of emotion. On any other day, "the spitter" and his heavy-handed antics could evoke strong retaliation from the best of us. At that moment, however, I had no fight left in me. As soon as the verbal lashing ended and the coast was clear, I gathered my things and cautiously made my way out of the empty classroom keeping one hand near to the wall just in case. I found the nearest latrine and dabbed the small cut on my right temple which would undoubtedly develop into a rainbow of a welt.

The crisp morning air had a soothing medicinal effect. A group of girls with curious disapproving stares spotted me. I nodded politely and quickened my pace hoping to avoid drawing attention to the throbbing lump dominating my temple. I was almost past the not so sweet sixteen gang when one of them called my name.

"Des!"

I turned around and scanned the perfectly pedicured group of about eight. They dissected me like a specimen straight out of fifth period science class, and that's when I saw her.

"Hope to see you this summer, Des," said Tessa, with a smile that nearly dropped me.

It sounded more like a question than a statement and I stood there stunned.

"Uh, sure," I said with a wobbly grin and as much pretend confidence as I could muster.

Just looking at her made me weak in the knees. Talking to her was even worse.

The group appeared to soften a bit with an endearing semi acceptance.

"You're Rudy Campbell's son," said the one with big teeth and blue ribbons tied in a massive bow around a stiff ponytail caked in hairspray.

"He's kinda famous," said a clone of the first one.

Blue ribbons piped up again.

"He doesn't look like Rudy Campbell. Rudy's handsome," she blurted, cocking her head and studying my face as if I weren't standing right there.

The group moved in closer to get a better look at me.

"Uh, yeah, that's my father." I said with the dullest of enthusiasm.

"What happened to your head?" said Ribbons.

"Are you bleeding? Does it hurt?" said the clone with bland concern.

"Oh that?" I said with a forced chuckle.

"It's nothing," I lied trying my best not to faint.

Our conversation evoked a hint of sympathy from this elite group of newly inducted seniors. Fake smiles let me know I was less detestable as when I had first appeared. In reality, I couldn't care less what they thought of me. They were phony, and in my opinion, Tessa didn't belong with any of them, but that was a whole other matter. The fact that Tessa knew my name had me loopy.

"Well, nice talking to y'all," I hurled with the same amount of fakeness slung at me.

Tessa watched me closely and dropped another smile bomb as I turned to leave, and I remained in a state of blissful shock for the remainder of the day. My head ached, but I didn't notice while I floated on cloud nine. Thoughts of her stayed with me and reappeared like clockwork where she filled every one of those long sleepless nights.

Two

My father, Randolph "Rudy" Campbell, headed teams of lawyers that stretched clear across the country. There were nearly two hundred attorneys, twenty-six partners and the rest of the pack nipping at ankles to make partner. Rudy, a master in the courtroom, had a sixth sense when it came to juries, knowing intuitively who was straddling the fence and how to manipulate them into submission. He once persuaded a prominent judge that a doctor's son was blinded by moonlight, the reason the boy's vehicle ended up in the judge's pool at three a.m. A shot of the vehicle, along with a slew of floating beer cans donned the front page of the Daily Charleston and that's when Rudy was hired. Things got cleaned up quick and shortly after, the young man was cleared of any wrong-doing and Rudy's pockets were stuffed with cash some of which was shared with the Judge. As the saying goes, Rudy Campbell could sell ice to an Eskimo.

The income from "lawyering," as Rudy called it, was far and wide and with it, he could buy just about anything and anyone. And so, he did. We lived on a five-acre estate in the most beautiful part of the Southern Carolina's called Charleston. It was a hike just to get from Johnson Road, which was our street address, to the front door of our home. The ghost-white old Southern mansion was featured from time to time in the local real estate magazines. It was something alright. Angel Oaks as old as time formed a tunnel over the long driveway and garnished the old mansion with a mysterious haunting beauty. Nestled inside the circular driveway, a cherub lined fountain pushed water to the sky amidst a fierce looking Archangel. The gardens around the fountain and the mansion were meticulously tended to and the aroma from hundreds of Magnolia Grandiflora wandered effortlessly throughout the stone walkways. My father purchased the run-down property from a debtor in 1947 for one dollar. Rumor has it, the man, accused of a murder-for-hire was one juror shy of an acquittal and it was Rudy's influence on that juror that secured the man's freedom.

The horse stable was a magnificent structure with ten 12x12 Tiger-wood stalls and ten Thoroughbred racers to match. If I entered the house by first passing through the stable, I had a good chance of avoiding the keen eye of my mother, Jean. The monster lump would undoubtedly invoke a barrage of questions for which I had little interest in answering. Jean had married Rudolph Campbell straight out of high school, handed off from one tyrant to another one in the making. Old southern aristocracy is a peculiar culture. Young women marry into wealth securing a life of prestige and comfort that sooner or later leaves them feeling void of self-esteem and independence. And so, it was with Rudy and Jean.

I had always loved the horse stable. The hustle and bustle of handlers and trainers, the smell of wood, hay and the rhythm of neighs was comforting and in sharp contrast to the relentless tension inside the mansion. Today, however, the stable was unnaturally quiet. I walked through the stable past the shower, tack and supply rooms toward the first row of stalls. Where was everyone? As I rounded the corner, I noticed an empty stall with the door slightly ajar. I made my way toward it and peered cautiously over the top rung. There I saw Rudy Campbell in the corner of the freshly hayed ground with a young woman. The duo rolled in ecstasy oblivious to the eyes that rested upon them as he ravaged her with abandon. She quickly turned and I recognized the curve of her face. It was Leslie, the daughter of one of the more tenured farm hands, Kendall Morgan. I froze.

Kendall Morgan, as big as a small bull, was a taciturn man with the personality of a Pine Hall Brick. Kendall and Leslie came to Campbell Mansion from Alabama in 1957, looking for work and whatever shelter they could find. Leslie's mother had abandoned her as a baby, and she grew up in the most difficult of circumstances. They came to live with us when Leslie was just seven years old. Rudy and Jean insisted I tutor Leslie because she missed at least two grades during the years she and Kendall drifted from town to town searching for work.

"Let's pretend we're Rudy and Jean," Leslie said once during a geography lesson.

Taking two of the crystals from the chandelier and placing them on her earlobes she proudly exclaimed, "Dah-ling, you must take me to dine at that new expensive restaurant!"

Flipping her hair behind each of her shoulders, she lifted her chin to proudly reveal her glittery diamond earrings. If I didn't go along with the charades, Leslie would start to cry and carry on, her wails echoing throughout the mansion drawing the attention of all within a three-mile radius. So, there I was pretending to be Rudy to appease her appetite for all the glory that wealth and privilege beget.

"Get us a reservation at the best table," I said in a deep manly voice to the make-believe person on the other end of the phone.

"My name is Rudolph the Red Nosed Campbell, and I'm a big smelly reindeer!" I said, emulating my father as a Christmas caribou with one outstretch finger at my temple.

Leslie roared with laughter at my antics especially when she learned Rudy had been listening on the other end of the phone the whole time. He had just begun to make a phone call when he heard my mockery and decided he would pay us a visit. He watched us from behind the coat rack while I strutted across the room wearing his Sunday best Richman Brothers overcoat dragging it along the floor behind me. Grasping the lapels with both hands, I straddled the center of the ottoman.

"Ladies and gentlemen," I began in syrupy sarcasm to the pretend crowd.

"Jean and I are so grateful you could all come," I said.

"Not really...I just invited you so maybe I'll get some business out of you," I said in a low whisper to Leslie.

Leslie played along to the pretend audience, nodding in joyous agreement to my remarks, her giggles rapid and continuous.

"You're so dear to our hearts," I said pounding my chest with a fist in overacted emotion.

"I can't stand any of you really. You're just a bunch of low-rate five and dimer's," I sputtered in a loud whisper, choking with laughter.

Leslie enjoyed the reprieve from studying, and I guess I did too. Up until we got caught. My punishment was to paint the fence around the stable for four weekends that summer while Leslie read *Teen Magazine* poolside. Every so often she would glance my way while sipping Sweet Iced Tea and fanning herself with the magazine. Ever since then, I was careful not to get into trouble on account of Leslie, locking myself in my room on occasion whenever she was bored.

Once she discovered boys liked her, however, I was off the hook. They found her extremely attractive, and this newly discovered knowledge became a powerful tool for Leslie Morgan. Leslie, now nearly seventeen, had the face of an angel and a wild, reckless spirit and she used what means she had to make her way in a world that had rejected her from the first entrance in. Campbell Mansion and all the prestige associated with it introduced Leslie to the kind of lifestyle she longed for and would pursue with a vengeance.

IN A SPLIT second, Leslie turned, and her eyes caught mine. I darted quickly back behind a post, sucking in all my breath. I inched my way ever so slowly back several feet keeping my eyes fixed on the stall. I knew if Rudy caught me watching them, I'd pay for it. I never crossed him.

Ever so quietly I backed up inch by inch until I was hidden behind the furthest stall nearest to the exit. I turned quickly, misjudging my position and ran into, nearly knocking over a supply cabinet filled top to bottom with hand tools and paint supplies. The cabinet swayed almost tipping over and I grabbed it with both hands cussing under my breath. I held it tight until it steadied, and the rattling ceased. I looked up just in time to see a can of spray paint swaying before it finally tumbled off the shelf. With more luck than skill, I caught it miraculously in one hand just before it hit the paver stone floor. Beads of sweat formed on my brow and I quietly pushed the can into my backpack. I heard the slam of a gate and I panicked. Sprinting out of the stable and over the shortest lawn to the left of the stable toward the safety of the woods I ran as fast as I could. I jumped over downed trees and pushed at branches that tore my skin and threatened to slow my pace. Off in the distance I heard someone call my name, but I didn't stop, I just kept going. By now, I was almost to the tracks.

Three

THE TRACKS WERE A PLACE no one would ever think of looking for me and I liked it that way. Still shaken by what I encountered at the stable, I tried to push it out of my mind. Tessa helped.

"Where've you been all day?" hollered Jean one afternoon as I tiptoed through the hallway after nearly a full day at the tracks. She poked her head out from around the corner just as I was about to hit the stairs.

"Playing ball," I said, contorting my face as though the inquiry was wildly ridiculous and inappropriate. I'd never get away with that if it were Rudy and a tinge of guilt raced through my mind but then quickly vanished.

Sports was considered an acceptable leisure activity for a spry young lad with a promising law career. Perusing street art at the tracks, however, was not. Over the years I had become good at sorting through what I shared with them. My time at the tracks was on a "need to know basis," and I had decided this was something they didn't need to know. I was free at the tracks, and I wasn't about to reveal my hiding place to anyone.

The double rail on either side of the median held lines of trains that traveled to and from major ports along the east coast. I scooped up pieces of fallen coal and swiftly tossed them into open cars while examining words and symbols of various shapes and colors. From the looks of things, these taggers were hard core street kids and nothing at all like the pampered crew at Rutledge Academy. Some considered the graffiti art but certainly not Rudy and Jean. At nearly eighteen, I could barely draw a stick figure thanks to Rudy.

I brought home my very own masterpiece on thick brown construction paper and couldn't wait to show them. The fifth-grade class spent all afternoon on art projects, and I cradled mine for three miles on the rickety bus trying my best not to ruin it.

"Look!" I shouted, holding it high above my head in the center of the kitchen. Rudy, stern faced, was on his feet in an instant. He snatched the picture out of my hands before I knew what hit me and tossed it into a small waste can.

"Art is for girls," he barked, grabbing his keys on his way to some fictitious evening appointment.

He slammed the door with a stifling bang as staff disappeared behind walls and Jean retreated to the garden and her roses. That was it for me and art even though I continued to be fascinated by it.

My future had been decided well before I had even grown a chin hair.

"My son's going to be a lawyer," Rudy announced at my tenth birthday party in front of a hand-picked crowd of twenty corporate types.

"What kind of law you gonna practice, kid?" fired Hugh Lamond while stuffing an enormous spoonful of potato salad in his mouth. Hugh, who I called Mr. Huge, gravely overestimated my scholastic pursuits.

I shrugged my shoulders without a word. Watching him eat was of far greater interest than our dull conversation. I was convinced Mr. Huge attended the parties just to stuff his face. He grazed his way to the food table for the fourth time piling a variety of desserts as high as an Egyptian pyramid. Conscious of his rather large frame, I liked to rattle him by pretending I couldn't say 'Hugh.'

"Mr. Huge," I said with the innocence of a small white dove. Is that your car?" I said pointing to a tiny red two-seater intended for someone with the body mass index of an eight-year-old.

"Yeah, kid, that's mine," he said inhaling an oversized cookie in one breath.

"It's fast," he warned with a sideways glance as though we were talking about a secret technology straight out of a Bond film. He paused to tend to a Jell-o thing smothered in marshmallow while I quickly vanished. I had had enough of the small talk and decided to grab a soda and climb a large oak tree where I could mingle with this clever crowd without their knowing.

I spotted Rudy's smoldering eyes fixed on a woman in a pink skirt. She could care less. The younger attorneys from the firm were nervous nellies around the big shots. Attentive and not nearly as tipsy as the others, it was clear they were all pining for promotions. I quietly giggled while sprinkling what was left of the soda on a bald guy tooting his horn to a group of uninterested suits. Jean, ever the gracious host was bored out of her mind. I too had grown tired and decided to make my way inside to watch TV.

I CROSSED the inner rails and stopped near a group of cars covered in graffiti. NYC glorified in pale blue covered an idle CSX. The bottom half of a Southern Carolina was marked in cartoon figures and obscure symbols, and a smiling Grim Reaper covered nearly three panels of a Norfolk Southern.

An ancient conductor lifted his hand like he knew me as the train inched closer at a pace slow enough to see his saggy eyes and weathered face.

"Hey there," he shouted against the train's churning engines while cupping his mouth with aged hands.

"You got any Camels?" he yelled.

"No," I said shaking my head.

"I don't smoke," I shouted.

With a toothless grin he waved, and I waved back as the line of twenty Norfolk's brimming with coal inched along rusted rails.

I continued east toward a poor section of Southern Carolina called Tennison Park. Tennison Park was mainly Negro folk and most of the families were single parents or elderly living in rundown houses and apartments called The Projects. The local government had turned its back on Tennison Park long ago in favor of the affluent communities of Charleston. The Negros who lived in Tennison Park didn't trust government or anyone of authority for that matter. It was carefully segregated, and I lamented that it was only a few miles of land that separated us. Charleston had privilege and Tennison Park was poor and forgotten, but in some ways, we were alike. I didn't like the influence my parents had on me and likewise the young Negros of Tennison Park didn't like theirs either.

I walked further and was startled by a monumental display of brilliant color that nearly took my breath away. It covered the entire lower half of the boxcar. Releasing the grip on my backpack, I let it drop to the ground somewhere behind me as I moved in closer. The sun broke through thick clouds high over Tennison Park illuminating the stunning display to full magnificence and I dropped to my knees. The crimson sky turned orange as it hovered over violent swirls of turquoise, green and blue. Rushing waves pushed silvery foam to tall peaks that cascaded into a sea that filled the base. Patches of yellow and white clouds stretched across the upper half from end to end and a border of black and gray framed the vivid colors creating a dramatic and compelling masterpiece. To the right, in what looked like a child had written its name for the very first time, 'Brando 7/4/67 T-Park'.

Unlike the other taggers, Brando had a unique gift. Had the mural been created by someone from Charleston or Mount Pleasant, it might be hung in the finest galleries in the South. But on these rusted panels, it would never have the chance. The mural pulled at me in a way I couldn't understand, and I didn't want to leave it, but as the light began to fade, the train's engine fired signaling its departure. A whistle screeched behind me, and I jerked as the axle and wheels turned in unison and the train began to move. I continued watching the mural as it moved through light and dark shadows that accentuated its beauty. With each minute the train gained speed and the mural grew smaller until it was nearly gone. The air was still and warm and I felt strangely sad and then suddenly desperate. My throat felt tight, and I reached for my backpack and started towards home. After only a few paces, I turned around and started in the direction of the mural slowly at first and then faster as the train reached full speed. I began to chase the car and ran for several blocks, finally catching up when it stopped at Crossing Station Fifty-Seven in the heart of downtown Tennison Park. Covered in sweat I threw off my jacket and reached for the can of spray paint. I shook it vigorously all the while keeping an eye out for local F.R.A. authority. On empty panels I sprayed *'Brando the Artist"* DC, 7/8/67. Somehow, I needed him to know it was good or maybe I just wanted to encourage him to be what I couldn't. Either way, I was satisfied.

It was well past dusk, and I was far from home and in a place where no one would come looking for a missing white kid from Charleston. Tennison Park was desperate, and I decided it was best that I find my way home by way of the tracks instead of the dark streets of Tennison Park.

TESSA'S ARRIVAL at Rutledge Academy brought a tidal wave of confusion

to many a dull mind. Locals were more than curious and somewhat intimidated by this attractive Yankee that had come all the way from New York
City. Word travels fast in small towns, and for those with inflated imagina-
tions and not much else to do, Tessa Rhodes aroused a bonanza of wonder.
Had she been part of a gang in New York? Does she carry a weapon? These
were the questions written on the faces of the townies who regarded outsiders with palpable suspicion.

"Why does your father play basketball with the Negros?" said the bra-
zen leader of a pack of girls that had purposely settled next to Tessa in the
Rutledge cafeteria.

Tessa contemplated the idiocy of the comment and its source. She knew
she was being set up by this pack of jackals that regularly roamed the halls
in search of easy prey. It was survival of the fittest in this new school which
Tessa surmised would make a fabulous feature story in *National Geographic*.

"Because he likes to. So what?" said Tessa, deliberately baiting the group
of petite cheerleaders along with one that was rather large and intimidating.

"But they're Negro," said the racoon with over-painted eyes, a near perfect half circle of brown eyeshadow that extended almost to the brows. No
kidding, Rocky, thought Tessa as she stifled an eye roll. She watched as the
group of six leaned forward anticipating her response, as if human existence depended on it. Tessa decided this dingbat group of Southern bells
needed educating and unfortunately, she would have to be the one to do it.
She sighed somewhat loudly before speaking.

"Doesn't your church teach that we're all equal in the eyes of God?" she
said to a stunned audience.

"Jesus was Jewish and not exactly white! Should he drink from the colored water fountain too?" she asked as the alpha of the pack stared intently
while twirling a lock of hair around one finger.

Tessa continued the crusade while the group marveled. Somehow this conversation was a monumental revelation to this sheltered group of hometown hypocrites. They finished lunches with eyes fixated on the new girl with the mind-blowing ideas. Tessa was already bored with this new school and this band of girls that controlled the entire political landscape of Rutledge Academy. They dominated every sport and social organization and managed these organizations with bigoted self-righteous attitudes. Tessa, however, was determined to take over the school paper and would mingle with this culturally challenged group as long as she had to in order to get what she wanted. They can keep the cheerleading, sports and social clubs, but the paper is going to be mine, thought Tessa. As editor of the school paper, she could influence the deluge of little minds that ran wild at Rutledge Academy. She missed New York and the ethnic mix of friends she left behind and longed to be rid of this unenlightened community of misfits. There was, however, one boy at Rutledge that appeared different from the rest.

She could feel him watching her as she sat in the small theater in the third row from the front. Somehow the gang of cheerleaders had decided on Tessa as their new project while they piled into the empty seats around her. It was embarrassing. Tessa didn't care to be associated with the jackals, but she needed to survive in this new school, so she went along with the charade. She looked around the theater and saw the boy with the sandy hair sitting by himself toward the back of the room. He looked away when she spotted him watching her.

"Aha! Caught you!" she thought.

Three minutes in, the lecture on Hellenistic Art had caused lids to drop to near closure. With fifty-seven minutes remaining, it was only a matter of time before the entire class were comatose. The instructor, a short little man with a medley of teeth fighting for space rambled incessantly in between high-pitched clearings of his throat. Professor Slaughter, the only one seemingly fascinated with Greek influenced art, periodically scanned the class through thick round spectacles simply to confirm the students were still there.

Tessa scribbled something on a notepad and crumbled it before it could be deciphered by her inquisitive neighbors. As Slaughter added more ancient fun facts to the chalkboard, Tessa whipped the crumbled paper like Babe Ruth to the boy at the back of the room while the Jackals contemplated her pitching arm. The cylinder startled him as it hit the edge of the desk before bouncing into the air.

He grabbed the wad and scanned the area to be sure he was the intended recipient before unraveling it with a half-smile. The instructions were clear. He should meet her by the bleachers after class which, as luck would have it, happened to be the last class of the day. Des nodded to the pretty Yankee, and she turned with a confident smile as her plans were set in motion.

When Des got to the bleachers, she was nowhere in sight, so he decided to circle them to be sure it wasn't some sort of cruel joke. As he neared the end of the long structure, he noticed across the lawn someone peeking from behind a narrow wall. She quickly tucked behind it as he approached.

"What are you doing?" he said.

"I'm hiding," she said from behind the wall.

"But you asked me to meet you here," he said.

"Not from you, silly," she said with a giggle.

"Oh. So, I suppose I should pretend to be doing something other than talking to someone that's not here?" he said turning away to peruse the sky.

"Yes, that's a good idea," she said.

"Are they gone?" she asked.

"Who?" he said.

"The barbie dolls that think they're my friends," she said.

"Oh, them. Yes, they're gone," said Des, scanning in both directions to be sure.

"Good," she said as she stepped out from behind the wall.

"They're trying to get me to go to cheer practice with them. They want to turn me into one of them," she said with a smirk while lighting a cigarette.

"Why do they want to do that?" he said.

"Because it validates their disfunction. If they can get someone like me to buy in to their prejudice B.S., they can justify it," she said.

"Well, why do you hang out with them?" he asked.

"Because I want something from them," she said.

"And you, too. I want something from you too," she said turning to look directly at Des while he struggled to keep from passing out.

They walked to the bleachers and climbed to the very top where they straddled a bench and sat facing one another. Tessa Rhodes was like nothing Des had ever encountered. She was bold, but kind. Pretty, but humble. She cared about people but not enough to allow herself to be pushed around. She was strategic and smart and knew what she wanted. Des Campbell liked her immediately and thought they would be friends and possibly more. After two hours of deep, meaningless conversation and several outbursts of laughter, they were both sure they had known one another in a prior life.

"What's it like in New York?" he asked.

"It's another world. My friends are the United Colors of Benetton, there's one of everything!" she said with a good measure of enthusiasm.

"But, every time my father gets a promotion, we have to move," she said with a frown.

"We were in New York for nearly five years," she said.

"It's not fair that I had to come here," she cried.

"I don't fit in," she said.

"I'm not like the kids at Rutledge, and neither are you," she said.

"How do you know?" he asked.

"I can tell by how you watch them," she said while playing with a piece of thread that had loosed from the wide rip on one knee of her jeans.

"I won't be here forever, and you probably won't either," he said.

"I'll stay long enough to finish general ed and then head off to law school somewhere," he said.

"Where will you go?" she asked.

"I don't know yet, but I hope it's far away," he said.

They walked and chatted nonstop about New York, Charleston and everything else under the sun. The chemistry was natural and being with Tessa gave Des a renewed hope in humanity. And pretty girls. When they got to her front door, he had a sudden urge to kiss her and he thought they actually might but with some awkwardness, they simply said goodbye. Later that night, he remembered she had said that she wanted something from him, and he hoped it might have something to do with his lips.

GERALDINE POWERS, the meanest of the jackals, was a large girl with broad shoulders and one uninterrupted eyebrow that hovered above piercing blue eyes. Powers sheer size and permanent scowl were enough to cause knees to knock in dimly lit hallways following evening sports practice.

After an armful of books were tossed out the school bus window, Powers was suspended for picking on a wobbly underclassman with a mouth full of metal. The books, having hit the windshield of the high school principal, bounced onto the hood of car number two sending it crashing into an elderly cyclist who landed head-first in a rocky ditch. After the cyclist was hit, the car flew across the road into oncoming traffic before clipping a fire hydrant that sent a deluge of water to the sky and onto the bus that had settled diagonally causing cars on both sides to come to a screeching halt. Someone called the cops and Powers' book tossing escapade turned into a full-blown crime scene. By the time the cyclist was transported to the nearest trauma center, a crowd of nearly one hundred soggy victims and spectators huddled on sidewalks while cuffs were placed on Powers' thick wrists. Needless to say, the unapologetic bully, was kicked out of Rutledge Academy, and ordained as the crux of all gossip for the next two months. Suspension for any reason meant the perpetrator was automatically booted from all sports and social programs. Powers, who could have easily been recruited without argument by Rutledge's football team, was immediately fired as editor of the school paper. This unfortunate incident left the door wide open for Tessa Rhodes who was thrilled to have a shot at controlling the published word at Rutledge Academy. She immediately went to work campaigning for the coveted position, and after having secured a prized interview with a local big shot lawyer, Tessa was nominated Editor in Chief.

The first order of business was to influence the fractured minds by publishing articles that would challenge the prejudicial strongholds. The jackals' control of the paper had resulted in years of bland articles featuring the most recent star jock and other loathsome characters. Tessa secretly planned to publish articles featuring outsiders from Tennison Park. She couldn't wait to display obscure faces on the front page which were sure to wreak havoc. She was determined to stir the pot and then watch the madness unfold at Rutledge Academy. First on the list was a boy named Brandon Thompson, an artist from Tennison Park. She first noticed him at the T-Park basketball courts. He appeared shy and was smaller than the other players, but he was also quicker. Brandon moved around the court easily, working his way through clusters of bodies with impressive efficiency. He lived with an aunt who considered herself an entrepreneur based on a lucrative weed business that catered to locals. Brandon was raised by a Negro named Barbara, after his biological mother was incarcerated and his father left town to pursue an extended vacation in Opa-Locka. Later on, Brandon was unofficially adopted by Barbara, who he considered his real mother. He moved in with Aunt K after Barbara, the only responsible caregiver, died unexpectedly. The mere tidbits Tessa knew about Brandon were enough to craft a stimulating article both intriguing and heartbreaking.

She waited until the game was finished and most of the players were gone.

"You're the artist," she said as she stood behind Brandon.

"What?" he said, turning around.

"Someone said you paint murals," she said.

"I'm a tagger if you consider that art," he said.

"Who are you?" he asked.

"I do. And I want to see it," she said.

"Why? What do you care?" he said.

"I need material for the Rutledge school rag. I want to interview you – and your aunt too," she said.

"Interview me! Are you crazy?" he said.

"No one from Rutledge wants to read about me. And as far as my aunt, she doesn't want her mug in no paper," he said shaking his head.

"You're barking up the wrong tree," he said.

"We aren't the kind of people Rutledge wants to read about," he said with a mocking laugh while pulling a worn sweatshirt over his head.

"Whatever you're smoking, you better quit!" he said with a smirk.

"Look, I know it sounds crazy, but you're exactly what I want. Rutledge, whether they know it or not, need to get to know people outside of the plastic bubble," she said.

"I want to publish articles that wake them up. They need to learn that the rest of the world isn't like them. I need you!" she pleaded.

"I already told you, but you're having trouble understanding," he said.

"Let me spell it out for you. I'm a TAGGER. If they know who's messing up the boxcars, I'll get arrested… get it?!" he said.

"Go find yourself some other Picasso," he said as he picked up a ball and brushed past her.

"Wait!" she said.

"Go back to the other side of the tracks where you belong. There's nothing here to write about," he said over his shoulder as he quickly left the court.

"HEY, WHERE'VE you been?" said Tessa as I made my way down Johnson Road toward home.

It was nearly a week since I saw Tessa Rhodes, and the sight of her instantly sent blood shooting through my veins at a rate so intense paramedics could have hauled me into the E.R. Besides food, she was the only thing I thought about twenty-four hours a day, seven days a week ever since the day we met. My mind was completely without focus and seeing her only added to the frenzy she created inside of me.

"I've been here," I said, sounding like a nervous fifth grader.

"We need to talk!" she said.

"Can you come by later? she asked.

"I'll be home by three," she said.

"Don't be late, Des!" she said, completely oblivious to the fact I would have given my right arm for just two minutes with her.

A feeble "ok" is all my mouth could generate even though she was now nearly ten paces down the sidewalk and couldn't hear me. Tessa left me mentally impaired, tongue tied, and confused and all at the same time. She had no idea the effect she had on me, and it was all but ruining my life. How was I ever going to get her out of my head?

I hurried home and showered like a madman then spent the next twenty minutes moving the part in my hair from one side of my head to the other then back again. I changed my clothes three times, and finally decided on an unassuming white T-shirt, and yesterday's trousers since Jean had lovingly ironed all the others leaving ridiculous thick creases down the shins. I practiced deep breathing exercises on the eight blocks to the Rhodes' house while trying not to sweat, and when I finally arrived, I discovered a note on the door with my name on it. In thick black marker she said she tried to catch me before I left, and she was sorry. She was meeting a boy from T-Park who had finally agreed (after a lengthy battle) to grant her an interview. She would phone me as soon as she got home. Exhausted from the traumatic buildup and subsequent letdown, I decided to go back home and pace near the phone where I would guard it like a Pitbull.

The book throwing incident was just too good not to print. Powers' loyal and slightly biased pals were aggressively opposed to it for obvious reasons. Tessa was giddy with anticipation. When the newspaper came out on Friday morning strategically three hours ahead of schedule, it was a grand slam without a single unconsumed copy. Powers in cuffs yelling at an officer with a slew of spectators on one side and an ambulance and occupied stretcher on the other was a photojournalism masterpiece. Some of the students appeared traumatized which only added to the jackal's PR problem. There was also a beautifully written article featuring Rutledge's *'most likely not to succeed'* female predator. And, with the jackal's façade all but shattered, Tessa was gleaming with the thought of next week's paper.

Brandon agreed to the interview on three conditions. One, she would use an alias, two, the photographs of the murals would exclude identifying characteristics. If she failed at either condition, he promised to decorate every inch of Parker Lane with florescent paint for as long as the Rhodes' occupied the home. The third condition had to do with the fact that she was pretty.

The idea for the article on Brandon helped sooth the aching heads of the jackals who were counting on a new controversy to draw attention away from Geraldine Powers, who endured minimal suffering while on house arrest for the remainder of the school year. Tessa would provide an update on the Powers situation with another article later on, but only after things calmed down and there was nothing else to write about.

She met Brandon at T-Park and decided if things went well, they could head to the tracks to see the murals. Tessa was equipped with an inexpensive Polaroid camera and a long list of questions in a small notebook, which were forgotten as soon as they began talking.

"Tell me about your life and how you began as an artist and don't leave anything out!" she said with an enthusiastic grin.

Brandon felt intimidated but at the same time, she was engaging, kind and so unlike the others from Rutledge, and he couldn't figure out why. No one from there had ever spoken to him let alone request an interview.

"Well, I live in T-Park with my Aunt K who's Negro. She's my adoptive mother's younger sister. My mother, Barbara, died when I was seven and there was nowhere else for me to go except to Aunt K's house," he said.

"Where's your real mother" she asked.

"She's in jail," he said.

"Where is your father?" she asked.

"I don't know," he said shrugging his shoulders.

"The last we heard, he had moved to Opa-Locka and was working as a street vendor selling biker jewelry and sponging off women," he said.

"When is the last time you saw him," she said.

"I don't remember much. I was a little kid," he said.

"My mother, Barbara, his girlfriend at the time, took me in after they broke up and he left me in the apartment," he said.

"I hadn't eaten in a few days and there was no electricity," he said.

"The landlord let her in to get the rest of her things and she found me. She took me to the diner on the corner and we ordered everything on the menu. It was great!" he said.

"Later we picked out some clothes, a few books and art supplies. We went to her house and that's where I stayed," he said.

"We spent hours doing art projects. She's the one that taught me to paint. She also made me go to school and was there waiting when I got out every day," he said.

"How did she die?" she said.

"She had a bad heart," he said.

"I tried to wake her up one morning, but she just wouldn't budge," he said.

"I stayed with her all night till Aunt K arrived the next day," he said.

"I'll bet you miss her," she said quietly.

"I miss her," he said shifting his eyes to something off in the distance.

Tessa had stopped writing after the page had become blurry. Why wasn't he bitter, she thought as she blinked away tears that had appeared suddenly. How could someone so kind be abandoned that many times and so brutally? She didn't know what to say next and was glad when he finally broke the silence.

"But I have Aunt K to think about, and I need to keep an eye on her," he said.

"She's not the best at picking out boyfriends and the one she has now is an overgrown idiot," he said.

"He knocks her around sometimes and that's when I step in," he said.

"But aren't you afraid?" she said.

"No, I'm not afraid," he lied.

"So, tell me about the murals on the boxcars," she said.

"Well, they're really fun to make if you don't get caught," he said with a short laugh that revealed an attractive smile and a dimple on one cheek.

"How do you begin?" she asked.

"Well, let me see," he said reaching into his pocket.

"First I make an outline with chalk, like this blue piece," he said.

"This chalk is special. It has pieces of silver in it and that makes it stick to the metal better," he said.

"If you look really close, you can see the specks of silver in the light," he said holding it up to the sun.

"Do you see it?" he said.

"No, I don't see it," she said shaking her head.

"Lean in and look really close," he said holding it steady as she moved in closer to examine the small cylinder.

"Get in closer! You have to look really, really close! There's just tiny pieces," he said.

Tessa cocked her head slightly and moved closer studying the small object intensely.

"I don't see it! Why can't I see it!" she said.

"Keep looking," he said as he turned the chalk horizontal in the sunlight.

"It's there! Right there, can't you see it?" he said as she moved in closer, now only inches from his face. He studied her eyes, the wisps of lashes that surrounded them and the crease in her brow as she tried desperately to locate the tiny pieces of silver that simply were not there.

When she was as near to the chalk as she could possibly be, Brandon swiped the blue stick down her nose with lightning speed which was followed by a belly laugh that could have woke the dead. Her reaction, a mix of shock and confusion were priceless as she jerked backward and studied him with two fingers resting on the bridge of her nose. Brandon managed a few shallow apologies in between cackles directed at the pretty girl with the blue streak on her nose. A devilish grin appeared, and Tessa decided Brandon should have a taste of his own medicine. They struggled over control of the chalk and who would wear more of it. She decided on a game of Tic-tac-toe and managed to get two x's and two o's on his cheeks. Soon, they both were covered in blue chalk and having the time of their lives. Later they cleaned up at the water fountain and headed to the tracks. Somehow along the way her hand ended up in his and the interview took a turn and began to feel more like a date. It was dark when she finally arrived home, greeted by a lengthy interrogation and shallow threat of grounding which was annoying, but well worth the time spent with Brandon Thompson.

Tessa's article on the Powers' incident had created nothing short of a frenzy at Rutledge. The Jackals were out for revenge, and a Trojan named David Crawford was furious that his mug and fourth quarter winning touchdown were somehow left out of the most recent edition of the Rutledge Bee. The new article about the unnamed boy from Tennison Park was also a huge problem. No one but Tessa could understand what he was doing on the front page even though it was clear he was remarkable and unusually talented. And, of course, there was more. Somehow the boy from T-Park with the courage of a thousand men had become more than just a friend. He had affected her in a way she couldn't understand. She smiled as she studied the piece of blue chalk before placing it inside a small jewelry box with other treasures known only to her. She turned the lever as a small white ballerina twirled to a familiar chime.

FOUR

THE SWELTERING CHARLESTON SUMMER was over in an instant. I checked myself for the twelfth time in the bathroom mirror before heading off for my final year at Rutledge Academy. Rutledge was founded on old money and support from wealthy contributors could be traced all the way back to the start of the Civil War. Many referred to Rutledge as lawyer prep school as most of the graduates headed straight to college and then on to Harvard, Columbia or Yale to study law and then join some of the most prestigious law firms in the country.

Most everyone in the Charleston community regarded my father, Rudy Campbell, with respect, but, as we all know, looks are deceiving. I couldn't wait to get off to college so I could be away from the charade. Rudy started off as a young eager lawyer and soon after graduation, started his own firm which grew in leaps and bounds attracting the most talented pools of astute graduates. I guess you could say he found his calling, but money and power change people and it was no different for Rudolph Campbell. The shock of seeing him with Leslie Morgan confirmed my suspicions and only added to the burden I felt in being his son. We never spoke about that day in the stable and I hoped we never would.

Rutledge Academy was bustling with energy on that first day back to school. There was an air of tension as I neared the archway to the main doors. Groups of students were talking intensely, and I had an odd feeling of being left out of something important. As I made my way down the main corridor, I secretly scanned the hallways for any glimpse of Tessa, but she was nowhere in sight. A lock of golden hair fell from where it had been meticulously placed, and I eagerly pushed it back in its rightful alignment. I couldn't wait to see Tessa, and this time, I had a plan. I was hopeful we would be in at least one class together. My strategy was to position myself one seat over, hopefully towards the back of the room giving myself clear line of sight yet out of view of an eagle-eyed professor. Private schools keep close tabs on their students and with class sizes at Rutledge no more than fourteen, it was nearly impossible to camouflage.

Good grades were important as they were my ticket out of Charleston. What I lacked in confidence, I made up for in smarts. I never really had to study. Learning came easy, and I had the ability to recall almost any lecture verbatim. The professors called on me whenever they were in a jam for participation. I had the right answers and elaborated to an extent that made them proud of their craft and proficient in the eyes of the other students. I gave them the satisfaction they longed for in a profession of limited regard and compensation.

How can anyone really know what or who they want to be until given the freedom to choose, I thought as I scanned the classroom. Looking around, I felt a hint of empathy for some of the others, knowing they too were corralled into careers they clearly were not cut out for. Some of them would barely make it out of law school and spend the rest of their lives trying to pass the bar and drinking heavily. I didn't have a Plan A or a Plan

B, for that matter and realized I needed to focus on some sort of career that would allow me to support a family. With brains like mine, it may as well be law.

I grimaced as the sound system's sharp feedback pierced our ears. The morning announcements usually began with an assault on our ear drums resulting in a nervous energy deep inside my gut. With certain predictability, Principal Gensler would begin with salesy comments about how exciting it was to be at Rutledge. The welcome to Rutledge campaign was designed to set the tone for the remainder of the school year. This time however, there was an anxiety to his voice that I couldn't quite put my finger on. He hesitated slightly and then began to stutter.

"L-ladies and gentlemen, I would like to welcome all of you to Rutledge Academy," he said.

He continued with a tedious welcome to new students and a familiar stern reminder of behavioral expectation, respect for authority and how those of privilege should conduct themselves. I let out a loud yawn by accident which garnished a few laughs from the back of the room and a grimace from the front. It was the same drill every year at Rutledge, and I couldn't help but think I was listening to the hypocritical voice of Rudy Campbell.

I positioned my body sideways on the chair as I anticipated the ring of the bell and conclusion of morning announcements. English Lit was clear across the campus and I had high hopes that Tessa would be in that class. She was a communications major and the editor of the school newspaper. Tessa had a reputation for being fair and giving equal coverage to both sides of an argument. That's why everyone loved her. Don't get me wrong, she was beautiful, but she had goodness too. People could trust that what she wrote was unbiased and sources remained confidential. If I didn't get into the classroom early enough, I would be resolved to take one of the few empty seats in the front. I preferred the back of the room where I could avoid participation while keeping an eye on Tessa.

I was up on my feet in an instant and then quickly shrunk back down as Gensler started to speak yet again. There was a short pause and then an uncomfortable clearing of his throat as he started.

"Rutledge Academy students, faculty and staff, it's with great sadness that I announce the passing of one of our own," he said.

That's when everything went completely quiet. The Klein twins in the back of the room ceased their endless chattering. The homeroom instructor put down the chalk and quit writing the day's lesson, turning his gaze to the speaker. Somehow, the quiet seemed to get louder. Attentive and anxious, we waited.

"Tessa Rhodes was killed yesterday evening in Tennison Park, just east of Charleston." Gensler cleared his throat nervously and continued with condolences to students and faculty.

I heard the echo of screams from a couple of girls down the hall. Gasps and the rumble of conversations exploded all around me. Shocked faces looked at one another in the hallways which were unnaturally quiet and eerie. Blood rushed to my ears and head, and I couldn't comprehend what I had just heard. The news tore through me like a bullet that traveled in one side and out the other. I could feel my face burning hot and my body convulse. I had no idea what was said afterwards. I moved in slow motion to the nearest latrine where I locked myself inside the first open stall for the next hour.

It hit me hard each morning. Sleep was the only reprieve from the stark reality that Tessa was gone. It was in the eighth grade when she moved to Charleston from New York City. Her father was recruited from a large bank headquartered in Manhattan to lead marketing efforts for one of the local Charleston banks. The Rhodes family had a contemporary, cool sophistication. Unlike most of the southern families, they weren't bigoted or afraid to interact with Negros. Segregation lingered heavily in the South even after the well-publicized *Kress Sit-In of 1960*, but it had no influence on the Rhodes'. Mr. and Mrs. Rhodes would walk to Rutledge on occasion when there was a school function, taking the longer route near Tennison Park. Mr. Rhodes, tall and lean, would take off his jacket and shoot hoops with young Negros from T-Park. Mrs. Rhodes, equally tall and pretty, would laugh along with the kids when Mr. Rhodes missed nine out of ten shots. He was terrible at basketball, but they liked him and trusted his authenticity. Mr. Rhodes would talk to you like you were a real person and not just a dumb kid, remembering details about your life not even your own parents could recall.

My heart ached, but I couldn't imagine how the Rhodes' felt. Rumors swirled throughout Rutledge and with each passing day, there was another new lie. Rumors of promiscuousness resulted in my sporting a black eye and fat lip on more than one occasion. I couldn't stand to hear Tessa's name dredged through the dirt unfairly by the elite southern hypocrites. The case dragged on for the next two years with a handful of suspects and no arrests.

FIVE

I WAS AN EIGHTEEN-YEAR-OLD FRESHMAN at College of Charleston in the fall of 1967. The local draft board, made up entirely of Charleston's elite, had me on a secret deferment list well before I had even enrolled.

"No son of mine is going to get slaughtered by a slit-eyed gook in Vietnam," Rudy barked as we sat down for dinner.

There was rumor that a disproportionate number of minorities and poor were placed first on the lists. Civil rights protests were happening all over the country, as well as in Charleston. Dr. Martin Luther King's visit in July of 1967 changed me forever and it was then I began to fully understand what it meant to be Negro.

"It's not right, that the Negros are chosen over the whites," I blurted.

The silent rebuttal told me my comment was not appreciated.

"Whatever gave you that idea," said Rudy impatiently.

"Well, that's what they're saying at school," I said earnestly as I poured milk into a glass.

"We're grateful that you're not going over there, and you should be thankful. And, you should think about getting a haircut," he barked.

My flowing locks, barely touching the tops of my ears were four inches shorter than I would have liked. The style automatically precluding any interest from the opposite sex, would disappear as soon as I left Charleston.

Jean was quiet, adopting Rudy's opinion as her own. She always found the most opportune time to depart and as expected, she got up to retrieve something from the kitchen that we surely did not need. Their lack of empathy for minorities was an outrage and only added to the disdain that lingered inside of me. The Orangeburg Massacre and the Vietnam War all had a profound impact on the students at College of Charleston. It seemed everyone I encountered was disturbed by these events except Rudy and Jean, who remained comfortably ignorant.

The final year at College of Charleston went by quickly. My LSAT and GPA scores afforded me easy access into the top three law schools in the country. Following a stimulating half hour with John Taylor, head of Legal and five hours with a clumsy law student from Buffalo, I chose Harvard Law. I walked the campus by myself and then settled in a coffee shop to watch students and faculty as they went about the day. On my fifth java I made friends with a senior law student named Josh Rolland who tripped on a chair leg and spilled his coffee all over my backpack. Josh turned twelve shades of red and apologized, I had calculated at least twenty times.

"I'm so sorry. I'm an idiot," he said pulling gobs of napkins from a dispenser.

He blotted the watery mess like a madman, leaving tiny pieces of napkin on everything he touched.

"Oh, no worries," I said, praying the brown liquid didn't make its way to the entry application I had been working on for no less than a year.

Josh proceeded to apologize five more times before the dispenser was completely empty and the sloppy mess cleaned up.

"My name's Josh, I'm from Buffalo," he said with an inviting smile and outstretched hand.

"How about I buy you a coffee?" he said desperately trying to make up for the disaster he'd created.

"Sure," I said.

"May as well have another one and make it an even six," I thought.

Josh also bought himself one which he clearly did not need. He was already a nervous wreck and could have used a chamomile tea and a couple of high dose sedatives. He plopped down across from me in the small booth with an arm full of law books and folders while swallowing a massive-glazed donut in record time. Apparently, we were now friends and Josh proceeded with a verbal dissertation on everything he knew about Harvard Law from the first day he set foot in Cambridge. By 11:00pm I had stifled three yawns and could barely keep my eyes from rolling backward. We walked across campus to Harvard Square where we shook hands and said goodnight. I barely took a step before he circled back to apologize one last time and I wondered what kind of law this bruiser was going to practice. Whatever his plans, I was grateful to have met Josh Rolland.

IT WAS Friday afternoon, and I made my way through the woods to the only place I felt at ease. Things were different ever since it was confirmed I would be going away to Harvard. I felt a lightness I hadn't felt all year knowing I would be leaving in the fall. There was little activity at the tracks and the warm breeze and sun on my shoulders felt good.

I kicked at an old soccer ball that had made its way to the median two boxcars from where I entered the tracks. I charged carefree down the center kicking the ball from side to side past ten boxcars till I came across a car with an open door. To the right of the door a striking and colorful display that I knew immediately was the work of Brando from Tennison Park. I positioned myself in the center of the open door and placed the ball directly in front of me. I backed up several feet and then with a wallop straight and hard, kicked the ball dead center inside the open boxcar.

I stopped to study the mural's distinct style before grabbing the rusted rails and climbing inside. Rays of light peered through the open crevasses highlighting several cans of discarded spray paint lying at the back of the car next to the worn soccer ball. Brando was the artist I had longed to be. Soon, I would head to Harvard Law, the most prestigious law school in the country, but I couldn't help but think that Brando, free to do what he loved, was the fortunate one.

Six

THE TRANSITION TO HARVARD dorms was easy, I felt just as alone and unsure of myself as I had at home. I was assigned a dorm in the section called Crimson Yard in a building called Wigglesworth. My roommate was a tall and shrewd kid from New York City named Bobby Jay Saltucci. Bobby made friends fast and quickly became the source for entrance into the most exclusive social functions in Cambridge. Bobby's good looks and confidence made him extremely popular with the ladies and I was excused from the dorm room regularly while Bobby entertained some of Harvard's finest.

"Hey Des, do you mind?" said Bobby Jay with a wry smile.

It was just past 9:00pm as he stood in the doorway cradling a cheap bottle of wine accompanied by a curly haired girl peeking from behind him.

"Oh, sure," I said, gathering up my things.

Lucky for me, the library would be open for another couple of hours. By now I was keen to Bobby's entertaining schedule and sure by the time I left the library, Bobby and company would be long gone.

"Des, I owe you one... or ten," he whispered with a wink and a pat on my arm.

As expected, when I arrived back at the dorm the honeymooners were nowhere to be found, and I had the booze-scented room all to myself. I didn't have any real friends at Harvard and the only one I did have had graduated in the spring. Bobby Jay regularly hounded me to frolic with him and the band of predators he hung with. This, I deducted had more to do with him wanting to salvage his tainted image brought about by his nerdy roommate. I dodged Bobby Jay and Co. as much as I could but knew sooner or later, I'd be forced to socialize with this Neanderthal group of up-and-coming professionals. I could hardly wait.

"SHE LIKES you," said Jean on a bitter day in February as we sat in a corner of the library.

A pretty brunette pushed a cart of books putting them back in their rightful place while stealing glimpses of us.

"No, she doesn't," I said.

"You're going to make a fine lawyer, Desmond Campbell," she squealed with a squeeze of my right arm.

"Any word on Tessa?" I blurted.

"They arrested a young man from Tennison Park, they're calling him the Boxcar Killer," she said with the emotional depth of a loaf of bread while examining her reflection in a small mirror.

"I think about her sometimes," I said lying through my teeth.

In truth, I thought about her every single day and her death had a profound impact that fueled my interest in criminal law.

"You'll find someone new, she said with a warm smile directed at the brunette who passed by yet again.

"We'll talk some more when your home," she said dismissing my grief with a light pat on the hand.

Jean checked her watch dutifully, buttoned her coat and with a brief hug, jovially said goodbye.

Her visits were always short and our conversations shallow. I suppose that was enough for Jean, but not me. I wasn't interested in a life of golf on Saturdays, country clubs and secret affairs. I watched her from the library's wide bay window make her way to a bright yellow cab and for the very first time, I felt sorry for her.

It was because of Tessa that I immersed myself in criminal law and devoured every book I could get my hands on. The library became my sanctuary, and I was regularly planted in one of the private study cubes till the wee hours of the night when the staff would reluctantly ask me to leave.

"Hi," said the pretty brunette named Leah.

"Um....we have to close up now," she said.

I gathered my things quickly as she walked me to the main entrance all the while trying my best to magically come up with something witty to say. I didn't want to sound like all the others I had witnessed trying to impress her, so as we walked, I said nothing.

"Thanks for the extra time," I said as she unlocked the door. She smiled.

Leah was still watching me when I turned around halfway down the hall, and I began to think maybe Jean was right about her.

Seven

Six years earlier...

It was my freshman year at Rutledge the very first time we spoke. After a series of hard- fought basketball games, I headed straight for the kitchen. With my bare hand, I enveloped a slice of chocolate pound cake and opened the door letting the cold air cool my skin. Grabbing a carton of milk, I guzzled it in record time and slammed the refrigerator door with a bang.

With the container secured, I stared down my opponent with fierce determination just as the doorbell rang. Turning sideways, I positioned it in both hands, one in front of the other and cocked my right wrist back fixating on my target. I faked a right pass as three defensemen attempted to block my shot and quickly jumped tossing the container high in the air and into the open can clear across the room. The cheers were deafening as I secured the state championship for the first time in the history of the school while my team lifted me high in the air floating over the adoring crowd.

The doorbell rang once more, and I leapt from the kitchen with a sea of fans charging after me. I ran through the grand foyer and half tripped pulling the heavy door with a quick thrust.

There she stood, pen and notebook in hand. Eye to eye, we examined one another for nearly a minute before she finally spoke.

"Hi, umm, I'm Tessa. I'm here to see Mr.", as she scanned a notepad.

"Uh, Campbell," she said.

"I, um, well, I'm a reporter for the Rutledge Academy and I have an appointment to... well interview him," she said as her eyes settled on something near my mouth.

She was pretty and I just stood there staring at her. Her eyes were a pale green and her lips pink with a cupid's bow. Long strands of silky hair flowed to her waist.

"Oh, come on in," I said as I pulled the door open.

With a shy smile she stepped inside peeking at the grand foyer. I ran my fingers through a damp crop of hair that flopped over one eye and batted like a madman at something on my chin while trying to smooth a badly wrinkled t-shirt.

As it turns out, Tessa was working on an article for Rutledge Academy newspaper featuring local business owners and their thoughts on hiring student interns. There was a good deal of interest by the Rutledge staff and student body in what Rudolph Campbell had to say. He didn't much like giving up unbillable time, but in the case of a beautiful young lady, he would most certainly make exception. Rudy entered the foyer from his office just past the grand staircase and greeted Tessa with a confident, flirtatious smile.

"You must be Tessa," he said as he shook her hand, holding on to it until she blushed.

"Yes sir," she said with flushed cheeks.

Rudy gave me a hard nod, an unmistakable cue to hit the road.

From my bedroom window I studied Tessa as she left the mansion while Rudy stood watching her. She turned around for only a second before her pace quickened and she dashed away. I wondered what they talked about for nearly an hour behind closed doors. Leslie Morgan wondered too as she marched over to Rudy with arms folded tight across her chest.

Later that night

"Who was that girl?" asked Leslie.

I closed the book and turned to see Leslie Morgan on my bed twisting a dark strand of wavy hair with pretend indifference. Mounds of shiny black hair accentuated the porcelain skin on her face and neck. Thick dark lashes lined soulful brown eyes. Leslie Morgan caught the eye of every male with a pulse, but her heart held firm to Rudy Campbell. Her hands rested palm to palm in a sideways prayer beneath her head as she finally looked at me.

"She's a girl from Rutledge that writes articles for the school paper," I said.

"Do you think she's pretty?" Leslie fired in rapid succession.

"Um... I guess so," I shrugged knowing exactly where she was headed.

Her eyes welled up and she grimaced with pain as tears rolled down her face.

"Does he li... like her?" she stammered.

I felt awkward, and all I could do was sit there. Rudy was the puppet master that pulled the strings of her heart and there was nothing anyone could do about it. The affair between them was no secret. The stable workers ignored blatant flirtations and Jean found ways to busy herself with a variety of distractions. I got up and moved to sit near her.

"You shouldn't bother with him," I whispered handing her a Kleenex.

I hated what he was doing to her. I wanted to tell her, 'Get away from here as fast as you can,' but, where would she go? She barely had an education and would only end up in trouble.

"But he takes care of me," she said in between short gasps of air while dabbing at her eyes and nose.

I took her hand and held it in mine. Leslie and I had a long history. Though she had tortured me plenty through the years, she was like a sister to me. We grew up together and our families were deeply tied.

"It'll be ok, please don't cry," I said.

I tried to cheer her up by telling her about all the boys at Rutledge pining to be my friend so they could meet my little sister.

"What do they say?" she said.

"They want to know if you're available. I tell them all to go pound salt," I said.

She seemed to like it that I was protective of her, and I was relieved when finally, she smiled. Rudy's face, however, bore a dangerous scowl as he entered the room. I dropped Leslie's hand like a hot iron and stood as she jumped from the bed. He put his arm around her shoulders and studied us with suspicious eyes that calculated our interactions.

Several weeks had passed and the intensity of their relationship surfaced to the point it was obvious to everyone, including Jean. Leslie was used to free rein at Campbell Mansion ever since she and Kendall moved into the small apartment over the garage. Until one day, everything changed.

Leslie tried her key in the lock of the main house before she realized it no longer fit. Rudy no longer pursued her, and someone had changed the locks.

"I hate you!" she said, pounding on the door with both fists.

Jean, arms folded, stood watching near a side window.

"That's what you get," whispered Jean as she watched from inside the quiet parlor.

That night Rudy arrived promptly at six. A kiss intended for her cheek was lost as Jean turned her head at precisely the right moment.

"What's for dinner, it smells delicious," he said.

"Lamb stew with collard greens," she snapped as we sat down at the long table.

She studied him as he ate. The lines on his face and neck appeared more pronounced. His hairline had deteriorated into a row of sparse gray seedlings that formed a ridge near the crown. She remembered what had attracted her when they first met. The sharp wit, relentless ambition and the promise of a good life. Twenty-five years had passed. He was a different person then, she thought. Honorable, kind and patient. She didn't know the stranger that now sat across the table from her.

"You will instruct her to leave the house," said Jean.

He stopped chewing and looked at her while I choked on a fork full of mashed potatoes that had lodged in my throat.

"Yes, I will," he said quickly.

"She is never to set foot on this property," she said without as much as a glance.

I watched wide eyed like a first-row spectator at Wimbledon as they volleyed.

He nodded quickly like a good boy to her demands and then quickly changed the subject.

In amiable charade they finished dinner and retired to separate rooms. I lay awake listening for any sign of reconciliation but there was no communication that night or for several weeks thereafter.

RUDY APPROACHED Kendall as he lifted soiled straw into a large wheel barrel.

"Kendall," said Rudy.

"Yes sir," said Kendall.

"You've been with me now for a long time and I value our relationship," he said while nervously jingling keys in this right pocket.

"What I'm trying to say is that, well, you and your daughter are like family," he said purposely avoiding saying her name.

Kendall waited unsure where this was going.

"Yes, sir," he said.

"As you know," Rudy continued, carefully.

"Leslie has become, well... bothersome to Jean," he sighed averting his gaze.

"Oh?" said Kendall.

Rudy, wasting little time, got right to the point.

"We think it might be best if she lives elsewhere or perhaps went away to college or something..." he said as he massaged fresh stubble on his chin.

"She's your daughter and Jean and I think of her as our own," he lied.

"But we think it's best that she got a place of her own away from here. Now I'm willing to cover the cost of tuition, apartment and incidentals, he blurted.

"However, we would like her to depart immediately," said Rudy.

Kendall could feel his heart race.

"But, sir, how... how will I tell her?" Kendall stammered.

"If she's not here... how will I look after her?" he pleaded.

"What if she..." said Kendall.

Rudy's demeanor darkened.

"I trust you'll handle this quickly and reasonably," said Rudy with a frown.

Without waiting for a reply, Rudy exited the stable. The veins in Kendall's neck swelled as white knuckles clutched the stem of a pitchfork. Shuffling to a nearby bench, he sat with a thud. He could feel his chest pumping and his hands tremble as he reached for a cloth to wipe his forehead. His mind raced for nearly an hour before he was able to move. Heavy legs pounded the floor as he shuffled through the stable turning off lights and closing doors before making his way to the small apartment above the garage.

Within a week Leslie moved into a studio apartment that bordered Tennison Park. It was affordable but not the kind of neighborhood Kendall would have liked. He worried what she might get into. She was young and he was too far away to keep a close eye on her. They called themselves The Freedom Movement. A group of twenty, revolving mix of runaways and anti-establishment squatters infiltrated a dilapidated house near the small apartment. Leslie, having no real structure, fit right in. Drugs and alcohol flowed freely and within six months, she was gone.

The funeral was horrible. I could barely stand to look at her pale and motionless and I hurried to the latrine on two occasions fearing I might hurl in front of everyone. Kendall sat alone in a corner of the stale room and spoke to no one. I watched him in between huddled groups of mourners that whispered softly. Kendall's eyes followed Rudy as he casually worked the room. Rudy and Jean spoke in brief, rehearsed sentences and commentary from other mourners sounded shallow and annoying. I was filled with grief, but what I witnessed in Kendall went far beyond grief. Kendall Morgan was furious.

KENDALL WAS ordered to deliver flowers to the Rhodes house again and he was tired of it. He would circle the block three or four times and make sure no one was home. Then, he would race to the local florist, buy a dozen red roses and hurry back to the house to drop the bouquet on the porch. Luckily, the Rhodes house was bordered by thick trees on both sides and a golf course in the back which provided Kendall easy access to the property. Once he waited all day for Mrs. Rhodes to leave the home. She returned just as he was about to step out of the vehicle. He quickly ducked back inside the car as she drove past unaware.

Kendall knew Rudy was after the Rhodes girl, but he needed his job, so he complied with the requests and did whatever was asked of him.

"Get roses for the Rhodes girl," said Rudy with a grunt.

Rudy didn't wait for a reply, but simply turned and exited the stable. It was the Fourth of July and Kendall had just returned from the cemetery like he always did on holidays and special occasions. With his beloved daughter deep in the ground, Kendall too was dead inside. He used to have someone to look after, someone to worry about and someone to love. Now, his only companion was the demon that would regularly nag at him to do things he didn't like to think about.

"Why don't you just kill her?" said the demon on that Saturday morning.

"Then you won't have to go there anymore. Afterall, she's the reason your daughter is dead," it said.

"Shut up!" Kendall said out loud in the stable.

"Just shut up!" he screamed.

"What?" said a young man hired to tend horses.

The boy walked tentatively around the corner to see what had caused all the commotion.

"Oh," said Kendall.

"I wasn't talking to you," he said quietly.

The boy was confused but returned to his chores without a word.

Kendall climbed into his vehicle and the demon went with him.

They drove to the Rhodes' neighborhood and did the usual drive by. Everything looked good so he raced to the florist to get the roses. When he got to Page's Floristry, the sign in the window read "closed." Kendall pounded on the door and waited, nervously scratching his arms. He thought he saw the shadow of someone inside the store, so he pounded on the door continuously.

"Ok, ok, I'm coming," said Donna Page.

She opened the door a crack and recognizing his face, let him inside. Kendall paid in cash just like all the other times and left the store in a hurry, however, when he got to his car, this time, it wouldn't start.

"No, no, no!" shouted Kendall as he turned the key in the ignition repeatedly.

But it was no use, the engine simply would not start.

"Now what are you going to do?" the demon said with a mocking laugh.

"Shut up!" said Kendall as he began to panic.

He raced back to the store and asked to use the phone.

"They're going to wilt," said the demon.

"No! It'll be fine," said Kendall shaking his head frantically.

It was nearly an hour by the time the tow truck driver arrived and was able to get the car started again. "You'll need a new alternator all right," said the mechanic.

"It should be ok for a day or so, but you'll need to get it replaced," he said while wiping his hands on stained overalls.

Kendall handed the man two ten-dollar bills, quickly jumped in the vehicle and raced to the Rhodes' house. The buds of the roses were now in seriously poor condition.

"They're wilted. You're so stupid," the demon said.

"Shut up!" screamed Kendall, sending drops of spit onto his front windshield as he sped through the quiet neighborhood.

Kendall drove past the Rhodes house two or three times and decided it was good. No cars, no lights, no sign of anyone. He would drop the flowers and get out of there as quickly as possible. He parked the car, kept the engine running and walked quickly up the side of the property to the left of the garage. He walked carefully across the driveway toward the front porch keeping a sharp eye on the windows for any sign of movement. There were no cars and no lights. The home looked empty, and he decided this would be an easy drop. Relieved, he placed the vase quietly in the center of the platform and rechecked the area before turning to leave. But just as he stepped off the porch, he heard the click of a dead bolt and saw the door quickly swing open.

"Who are you?" she asked.

Kendall was stunned and didn't know what to say or do next.

"I... uh, I was asked to drop these off," he said.

"By, who? Who asked you to do that?" she demanded.

Tessa had suspected the bouquets were from the creepy old lawyer she had interviewed for the school paper. He had been stalking her ever since.

Kendall began to sweat. She stepped out onto the porch and came closer looking directly in his eyes.

"Did you leave all of the other bouquets?" she asked.

Kendall didn't answer but just looked at her.

"You'd better tell me or I'm going to call the police," she threatened.

"Get rid of her!" the demon said.

"No!" shouted Kendall.

"Please, don't! I'll get fired," he begged.

"What!? I don't care... I want to know who put you up to this. It's Rudy Campbell, isn't it?" she demanded.

"Ok, ok, I'll tell you!" cried Kendall.

"Just give me a minute," he said holding his chest.

"Are you ok?" she said as she closely examined his face.

"You're turning red!" she blurted.

Kendall could feel his heart pound uncontrollably as the blood raced through his veins. He stumbled to a porch chair and grabbed the arm to steady himself.

"Stay there! I'll get you some water," she said.

She raced into the house as Kendall tried to gain control of himself.

"She can identify you. Now you have no choice but to get rid of her," the demon said.

"Hurry, you don't have much time," it said slyly.

"Ok, ok, yes, ok," said Kendall in between shallow gasps.

"Here you go," she said as she stood at the entrance with only minutes of her life remaining.

Kendall stood slowly. Seemingly grateful as his hand lifted reaching for the glass, but without warning, it quickly veered to the right bypassing it altogether. With one giant hand he enveloped the base of her neck. He grabbed her so quickly and his grip so tight, there was no time to flee. Now clasping her throat with both hands, he squeezed as hard as he could lifting her up off the concrete while his face burned and eyes bulge. She flutters briefly without a sound as the glass shatters on concrete sending shards exploding beneath them.

Dripping in sweat, Kendall holds on tight for minutes before slowly guiding her limp body down onto the entryway where she lay in a heap motionless. Racing to the car, he backs into the driveway as far up to the house as possible. He quickly flings open the trunk and runs to the house, lifting her lifeless body and dropping it down into the deep cavern. Kendall slams the front door and quickly kicks pieces of broken glass from the porch. He throws the wilted roses into the backseat as he tears away from the home as fast as he can.

Sweat pours from his face and stings his eyes as he dashes from the quiet neighborhood toward Tennison Park. He races through town turning onto a desolate road lined with abandoned warehouses and cracked parking lots. Deep potholes on deteriorated pavement cause him to straddle a narrow section of the road that runs for two miles and ends at the tracks. Kendall turns the wheel to the right and sails over four rows of railroad tracks and onto a dead-end street before he slams the brakes causing the nose of the car to dip slightly. Putting the car in reverse, he backs up and then pulls forward onto a gravel path that runs the length of the tracks making his way deep into the woods. He finds a shallow clearing and hides the car behind a wall of thick trees. Kendall knows he has to hurry. It is now late afternoon and soon the trains will pass through Tennison Park before making a final stop at Charleston Station. Kendall quickly parks and runs into the woods through thick brush and choking vines. Thorns rip holes in his arms and face in the stifling heat as he pushes through thick terrain. Tearing at the tangled wall with his bare hands, Kendall desperately searches for a secluded place deep in the woods. He comes upon a small opening to the right where a large purple Willow towers to the sky. Its strong flowering vines stretch down into the ground creating a tent-like fortress surrounded by thick brush and giant thorns. The tree's twisted limbs are covered in green leaves and small purple flowers which join the soft ground and secure the enclosure with its sturdy twisted bars. The Willow's fragrance, like sweet ripe fruit fills the isolated encampment perfect for masking decay that will soon permeate the air.

"Put it under the tree," hissed the demon.

"No one will ever find it there," it lied.

"Ok, yes, ok!" said Kendall whose face and arms are now streaked and dripping with blood and sweat.

Kendall races back to the car and thrusts open the trunk, sliding his arms easily under Tessa's small torso he lifts her. With his face only inches from hers, he hesitates for only a moment before noticing subtle movement beneath her lids. He freezes and stops to study her eyes, leaning in closer unsure of what exactly he saw, and just as he's about to lift her from the trunk, she suddenly opens her eyes. Wide. Tessa is alive!

Stunned, he drops her onto the trunk floor while slamming his head into the latch of the trunk's heavy lid.

"Ugh," he cried.

The hit was hard, and the sting, like a dull knife thrust into the back of his head. Kendall winces as he grasps the throbbing ache, but before he can recover, she plans her escape. Tessa lifts her knee quickly and with all her strength, thrusts her foot hard into Kendall's jaw causing his head to jerk backward and his body to reel out of control and away from the vehicle. Losing his balance, Kendall stumbles, tripping over his own feet as he tumbles down onto a small patch of gravel while Tessa desperately fights to escape the deep trunk. Her head feels heavy, and nothing makes any sense. Why is it so hard for her body to move and where is the monster that towered over her just moments ago? Tessa reaches for the rim of the trunk but for some reason, her strength is diminished and climbing out seems like an impossible task.

Stunned and shaken, Kendall breaths in heavy gasps as he strains to regain control. He swipes at small pebbles that have lodged in his palms all the while keeping his dark eyes fixed on the trunk. He manages to get onto his knees and lunges for the car's fender lifting his heavy torso while Tessa lifts herself upright inside the trunk. She begins to cry realizing she's in a deserted place and alone except for the monster and begins screaming for help.

The incident has made him angry, and with labored gasps, Kendall grabs ahold of her, locking his hands on her arms and with brute force, whips her out of the trunk. He nearly drops her as she is dragged across stone as sharp thorns tear her skin. Tessa is no match for Kendall's bull strength. He pulls her roughly through the bush, her screams echoing through the trees. His massive hand slams hard over her mouth as her struggling frame is pummeled through thick brush toward the Weeping Willow.

Under the tree Kendall finishes what he started. He tosses her to the ground and straddles her placing his hands again around her small neck, this time unmoving as her eyes bulge and then slowly fade. The heartbeat underneath him is no longer felt. And when he's done and sure she can no longer fight, he drags her to the base of the Willow Tree. Her frame is small, and her face is serene, almost peaceful as if she's asleep. It's quiet at the tracks except for the periodic squawk from a crow that calls from above. Kendall covers his face with both hands.

"I'm sorry," he says quietly to the dead girl at his side.

In a moment of regret, he brushes the hair from her face and places her hands one on top of the other while he quietly sobs. His body begins to shake uncontrollably with the realization of what he's done, however the screech of a train's whistle is loud and brings him to his feet instantly. Pushing his way out, he yanks at branches as he races from the tree clawing his way through the woods. He darts to the right for several yards and breathing hard, stops to scan the unfamiliar terrain. His mind is racing, and he's confused. The train's whistle, much louder now, prompts him to dash to the left and then impulsively to the right again. Finally, out of breath and confused, he is forced to stop and rest. His large frame is unused to moving fast and he's exhausted. Gasping for air with his hands on his knees, Kendall hears a rustling in the brush, and he freezes. Out of nowhere a young man darts towards him. The boy looks as though he's running from something and without looking, slams hard into Kendall's torso. Their eyes meet for only a second before the scared boy quickly dashes off into the woods. Kendall begins chase but then realizes there's no time, he's got to get out of there and fast.

EIGHT

Detective, Ray Combs had been with the Charleston Police Department since he was twenty-two years old. He grew up in Tennison Park and cleaned offices at C.P.D. after making friends with a rookie officer working night patrol. The officer shared his lunch with Ray who scarcely had a meal a day and that's how his career started. Now in his late fifties, Ray had worked his way through school and then up through the ranks of the C.P.D. He was invaluable when it came to solving crime in Tennison Park. He knew the city and the people, and they respected him but more importantly, it was trust that won their favor. For Combs, policing 101 was simple, secure the trust of the people and you'll get what you need for a conviction. In exchange, you protect them, no exceptions and that's how an officer becomes a detective.

Combs had his eye on five suspects, two white, two Negro, one anonymous and all are male. It was 8:30pm on Friday night and Combs sat at his desk, scratching the nubs on his chin retracing Tessa's steps while staring at the gruesome photographs spread out before him. Why was she found so close to Tennison Park? She didn't live there and as far as he knew, didn't hang with anyone from there. Her body was laid under an enormous purple willow. Thousands of flowery lavender strings cascaded over the twisted dark wood like a mystical giant protecting a small corpse. She was carefully set on her back with her hands folded one atop the other. Tessa wasn't sexually assaulted, but her neck was broken. Why was a young woman with no enemies murdered so brutally and then laid out so carefully? Almost as if he were sorry. Combs was stumped and frustrated. It had been ten weeks and pressure by the southern elite was mounting along with internal pressure causing intense anxiety. Combs stretched backwards cupping his hands behind his head for several minutes before unlocking the bottom right desk drawer to retrieve a small bottle of scotch whiskey. He squinted as the smokey liquid burned his tongue and throat anticipating the subtle buzz he craved at the end of yet another frustrating day. The photographs, no longer shocking, were gathered in a folder and then locked inside a drawer with a set of keys that he shared with no one. He placed the Whiskey back in the drawer, tucked a picture of Tessa into his front pocket and reached for his jacket.

Nine

Frowning, Bobby Jay lay on his side, one arm propped holding his head as he watched me study. I ignored several loud sighs before he suddenly jumped from the bed. He grabbed the book underneath me and slammed it shut, tossing it clear across the room.

"It's Saturday night, we're going!"

I knew he meant it this time and wasn't going to let me off the hook. Bobby shoved my jacket at my chest and off we went. The Stones' "Paint it Black" exploded from large speakers positioned in each corner of the room as a haze of smoke lingered throughout the museum's bar. I wasn't ready when he pushed a tall Guinness at me spilling it down the front of my shirt. I brushed at the foamy liquid turning away from the high rollers who were part of the "Deferment Club" that Bobby hung with. Eventually, I made my way over to a corner of the crowded museum to observe the steady stream of ladies eager for Bobby's attention. He had it down pat. He would talk to one while scanning the room for two or three others. Bobby didn't have to work hard at it, they all liked him, and he knew it. He'd have his pick and that was that. They were all beautiful but nothing like Tessa. These ladies were spoiled and aggressive, and I couldn't wait to get out of there. I made my way out of the bar to a semi empty hallway stopping to admire the canvasses and detailed inscriptions chiseled on brass plaques. An abstract by someone named Castle reminded me of the boxcar murals and Brando, who was much better than any of the artists on these walls.

Ginny Parks spotted me and staggered over, hugging me from behind. The alcohol and cigarettes on her breath rancid as she tried to lure me into taking her home.

"Des," she murmured sloppily. "Let's get out-a here, and go someplace funner," she said with a drunken giggle and arms deadlocked around my torso.

I reached for the wall to keep from stumbling while I worked to dismantle this lonely female octopus that had suddenly taken a liking to me.

"Ginny, not tonight," I said with more disgust than I had intended to reveal. We struggled for several seconds before I was finally able to literally get her off my back.

"Come on, Ginny, leave it alone," I said like a doting parent trying to reason with an unruly toddler.

She made one final attempt to seduce me and with minimal effort, I was able to push her away. She hit the wall with a soft bump and with a bruised ego, she became enraged.

Ginny began with a verbal attack and medley of profanity hurled at me as Bobby Jay and the high rollers wobbled over taking in the evening's entertainment for which I had a starring role.

"You're probably gay!" she screamed as she tossed the contents of her drink stinging my eyes and face before turning with an angry glare to nestle into Bobby Jay's open arms. The power couple and their entourage headed back to the bar and I, to the nearest latrine.

I splashed cool water on my face and reached for a hand towel to dab at the sticky liquid sprinkled over my skin. Grateful to be away from this charming group of intellectuals, I had no doubt I'd be long forgotten by the time they ingested the next round. By the time I cleaned myself up, the high rollers had made their way outside, stumbling to the next watering hole twenty yards up.

Two of the imbeciles stopped to ogle a couple of girls sitting outside Mason Street bar. Kevin Jones had invited himself to sit next to one of the girls, Leah, whom I recognized from the library. Kevin was a member of Harvard's International Student Law Program and the offspring of a wealthy British family from Buckinghamshire. They made their fortune in heavy equipment and supplied product to the US Military in support of our efforts in Vietnam. Needless to say, Kevin Jones was fabulously unpopular amongst the Harvard student body. I caught up to them in time to get a front row view of Jones' fine British upbringing.

"Wow, you look nice," said an inebriated Kevin, reaching for Leah and pulling her tight while his bloodshot eyeballs fixated on her torso.

Leah Robbins, a petite brunette with brown eyes recoiled in disgust. A history major, Leah was quiet, intelligent and just plain gorgeous. Throughout my time in the library, I noted countless sets of eyes including my own peaking over books as she passed through the aisles.

She continued to shun Jones as I moved closer to the group. Oblivious, Kevin kept at it as she tried unsuccessfully to get away. With large, thick arms, he continued to pull her close until she was stuck in between Jones and his ape like cousin, Mark Stone.

"Why won't you give me a kiss?" he said in an aggressive whisper.

The thug pulled her down effortlessly as she attempted to get up burying his face in her neck as his other hand massaged her waist.

"Hey, Jones," I said resting my arms on the ledge of the rail. The lady clearly wants to be left alone."

"Piss off," Kevin snarled, turning to Leah again for the affection he craved.

I knew I'd have to fight him in order to get him away from her and I wasn't looking forward to it.

"Come on fat boy, let's go," I said with a smirk.

He turned sharply.

"Who you callin' fat?"

"You, fat boy."

It was now serious. The challenge flag was thrown and with a flushed face he stood with the other bookend in tow.

"Campbell, I'm gonna mess you up," he growled.

I stood ready with fists high in a wide stance. All 154 pounds of me trembled, but I kept my eye on him and my footing agile.

Kevin Jones was a big boy with clearly more fat than muscle and at two hundred and fifty-five pounds, he was nearly twice my weight. My plan was to use his drunkenness to my advantage and wear him out.

He circled with his fists ready to strike.

"Knock the piss out of 'em," shouted Mark.

Kevin lunged with a sloppy right hook, missing me by a mile. He fell to one knee with a loud groan. Rising wobbly, he turned with an angry scowl and wiped his mouth with the back of his hand. Again, he lunged and swung with a wide right directed at my cheek. I cocked my head, missing his fist easily. It was clear, his weight and drunkenness hindered his ability to move and he looked like at any moment, that he might be sick.

I jumped past and got behind him coming in close to the back of his right ear, "Come on fat boy," I said, smugly while stealing glimpses of Leah. He didn't turn around but just stood there with his back to me sweating and breathing heavy. I felt he may be conquered. Perhaps he had finally had enough. I came in close again goading him by flicking his right ear with my index finger.

"Hey there fat boy."

But he wasn't done... he wasn't done at all.

I came in close again for another go at it, but he surprised me with a sudden twist of his torso. With all his weight behind it, a sharp elbow landed straight and hard in the center of my gut. The impact knocked the wind out of me, and I immediately doubled over clutching my stomach and gasping for air. I stumbled forward and then backward. When I was finally able to stand upright, he was ready and hit me hard with his massive fist right between the eyes. I was out cold.

When I woke, I was in Leah's apartment. She dabbed at my eyes with a cold compress while she studied my face. My head throbbed and a sliver of sight told me my eyes were nearly swollen shut.

"You look horrible," she said shaking her head.

"Thanks," I groaned.

Having her tend to my wounds made it all worthwhile. Good Lord, I loved looking at her.

"How's the other guy?" I said with a wobbly grin.

"Doesn't have a scratch on him," she giggled.

"Bet he won't mess with me again."

"Yeah, he learned his lesson," she quipped tossing a towel on my face before leaving for more ice.

I spent the next several weeks at Leah's apartment, stopping at Wigglesworth only briefly for clean clothes and law books. We spent the summer exploring Cambridge's museums, historical sites and each other. I never said it and neither did she, but we both knew we had fallen in love.

TEN

Detective Combs pulled into the lot at Rutledge Academy and reached for the glovebox to retrieve a small bottle of bluish liquid next to the Scotch Whiskey. He pumped twice in his mouth and checked himself in the rearview mirror before exiting the vehicle. A shiny gold cross hung from the mirror reflecting slivers of light that danced over the weather-worn dashboard. Combs, knowing exactly what he would encounter inside the school, whispered a short prayer. "I need you with me in there, he said with a sigh. This place is like a rose. It looks pretty but there's thorns that leave deep cuts," he said as he turned the car off and thumbed through a file on the passenger seat.

The old Chevy Impala made quite an impression parked between a couple of Mercedes. The rest of the cars in the lot resembled the luxury book ends on either side of him. Ray couldn't help but notice the students perusing the worn-out Chevy, staring at the bomber with creased brows like a bad accident difficult to view yet impossible to turn away from. "Mind your business," he mumbled while eyeing one student that was especially rude. Combs exited the vehicle and followed the students as they made their way across perfectly manicured lawns through a stone archway into Rutledge Academy.

They were gathered in groups of five or six in their emblem blazers and white collared shirts and as he neared the entrance, he wondered which one was Tessa's killer.

A toothpick dangled lazily from his mouth as he stepped inside the main corridor. Combs felt instantly out of place amongst the white privileged student body just as he had many years ago. He began working towards his degree in criminal justice at Piedmont Community College. It was more cost effective for many of the affluent families in Charleston to send their sons and daughters to P.C.C. to complete general education requirements before continuing to professional studies. Combs never forgot the blatant stares and mocking he endured from the wealthy Piedmont students. He did his homework and slept in the coat room at C.P.D. for two years. He owned two sets of clothes, both rags including a beat-up bomber jacket the rookie cop had given him. The Stedman brothers sat behind him in business law shooting spitballs at his hair and jacket to the amusement of the rest of the class. Poor and Negro, Combs had been bruised on more than one occasion. The bullies knew Combs, being a criminal justice major, couldn't get into any kind of trouble, so they kept at him freely throughout the two years at Piedmont.

He stopped just inside the main doors to admire the cathedral ceilings, rich mahogany woodwork and finely painted walls and ceilings. Portraits of distinguished faculty and wealthy contributors stared down from ornate gold frames hung side by side down the long hallway. Antique handrails illuminated bright white in the morning sunlight. Tennison Park lockers were a far cry from Rutledge Academy's which were tall, wide and lockless. Every inch of the interior space looked sparkling clean with hallways spacious and free of graffiti or garbage. Not one of them seemed to notice, thought Combs. This is all normal to them, he mused. Combs followed an arrow to the right pointing the way to the Principal's Office.

From his office, Principal Gensler greeted Combs with a toothy smile and nerdy thumbs up while cradling a phone tight to his cheek. He paced behind a large wooden desk with pretend interest in the phone conversation while eying Combs. Detective Combs chose a seat in direct view of Gensler while a young secretary handed him water in a paper cup. Combs wanted to know everything he could about Rutledge and its overrated leadership team as he understood the welcomed visits would be few.

"Thank you," said Combs.

"Are you here about the Rhodes's case?" the secretary inquired nonchalantly, acting as though she didn't already know.

"Well, I'd rather not comment, if you don't mind," said Combs with a polite smile.

"Oh, I understand completely," she said with enough drama to fill a small theater.

Combs was hoping she would leave it alone, but no such luck.

"We don't think David Crawford did it, just so you know. Not that it matters, but he's my second cousin on my father's side," she said with pride. Combs wondered about the pride thing. Afterall, David Crawford Jr. was well known by C.P.D., having been a frequent flyer on many a suspect list. Most people with half a brain would thoroughly distance themselves from the sweet and cuddly David Crawford, Jr.

"David is big baby really. He couldn't hurt a fly. Still sucks his thumb when it thunders," she said stifling a giggle with one hand over her mouth.

"Good to know. Thank you for sharing that," said Combs with the realization there was a lot more fruit in these trees than he previously thought.

"You're very welcome," she said with sincerity as if the information were of material benefit to the case.

Combs and Gensler continued their assessment of one another from a distance until Gensler finally emerged beaming with a painted-on smile and extended hand. The handshake, a bit too long made Combs increasingly suspicious. The polite niceties were brief as Combs sat down in Gensler's cluttered office while Gensler stuck his thick head out the doorway with a grand announcement to the staff of one to hold his calls.

Combs wondered who might be calling as the phone never rang the entire twenty minutes as he sat waiting.

The office, a shrine to self from the beginning of time, was a mixture of dusty remembrances, service awards and dated photographs. The stale and windowless office was a fire hazard in desperate need of a thorough power washing. Combs was certain the Rutledge maintenance budget had ended here. From the looks of things, Gensler had spent his entire career in this office doing exactly what the board of directors told him to do.

With creased brow, Gensler got right to the point.

"We have good students here detective. Good students," he said with overacted emotion.

Combs wondered who exactly he was trying to convince.

"We've never had an incident like this at Rutledge," he said with wide eyed bewilderment.

Combs, having pulled the incident report on Rutledge, knew he was lying. It included several assaults, a couple of vandalism convictions and one alleged rape. All of it spanned a ten-year period. The rape victim, who refused to cooperate, was too scared to testify and the case against her accuser, David Crawford Jr., was dropped. Combs knew exactly what kind of students were at Rutledge. He had fingerprinted several of them.

"I and the board, well, we're deeply troubled by it," Gensler said with the sincerity of a ventriloquist's puppet. We teach kindness and empathy here at Rutledge and I guarantee once your due diligence is complete, ANY suspect related to Rutledge Academy will be cleared," he gushed with the desperation of a used car salesman.

Gensler continued with his meaningless lecture for what seemed like an eternity. He paced continually throughout the rehearsed speech which grew increasingly dull by the minute. Finally, Combs had had enough. He purposely checked his watch and eyed Gensler with a weary gaze.

"Now I don't want to disrupt the students and faculty any more than we have to. As I'm sure you can understand, our funding and community support depend on our good reputation, a reputation we have sustained for decades," said Gensler with fake confidence.

"Mr. Gensler," said Combs, picturing his hands around Gensler's throat, stood to face his opponent eye to eye.

"I am completely aware of your uh…concern for the school's reputation and can appreciate your protectiveness of the student body, as well as the financial supporters. However, I will do my job," shouted Combs.

Gensler attempted to start again but was quickly cut off.

"In case you haven't noticed, Combs roared. A young woman is dead, and I intend, come hell or high water, to find out who killed her."

Gensler shrunk into his seat and reluctantly answered all the detective's questions with scripted answers before handing him off to a colleague who promised to supply him with names and contact information of Tessa's friends and others. Combs had little faith the information would be of much use.

Combs returned to his office frustrated. Arms crossed, he stood perusing the names, and notes taped to a chalk board with a picture of Tessa centered. Tomorrow he would visit David Crawford, Jr. and he was looking forward to it.

David Crawford Jr. was a defensive lineman for the Rutledge Trojans. Friends of Tessa revealed David had been stalking her since the eighth grade right up to the week before she was killed. Tessa had spotted David darting clumsily behind trees and buildings. David, now at 6'2" and 238 pounds was as difficult to conceal as a Rhinoceros. Tessa had described it as a silly crush, but Combs wasn't so sure.

Combs was escorted by David Crawford Sr. into the large formal living room where David Jr. was already seated. A heavy-set kid with mild acne and an unflattering crew cut sat nervously on the edge of a high-back chair. Combs noticed heavy beads of sweat forming on his brow and wondered why David was already so nervous.

"How are you, David?" said Combs extending his hand.

"Good sir," stuttered David, shaking Combs' hand awkwardly.

"Trojans are eight and one from what I hear. Pretty nice work David."

"Thank you, sir."

"You can call me Ray. We're friends."

Talking football helped David relax and appeared to put him at ease and that's exactly where Combs wanted him. Crawford Sr. stood close by eager to run interference should the conversation go in an unflattering direction. When it came to the topic of Tessa, it was apparent Junior was well coached.

"David, can you tell me about your day on July 4 from start to finish? For example, what did you do, where did you go and who were you with?"

Combs was jotting down notes that consisted of several "I don't recall's" all the while David was interrupted periodically by Crawford Sr. answering for him.

"Mr. Crawford, if you would please," said Combs.

"Well, I'm just helping my boy recall, after all, it was several weeks ago, and he's, well, he's under a lot of pressure between his athletic commitments and schoolwork. My boy has a solid B average; certainly, you can understand," said Crawford Sr.

Combs was confident the "B" average was most likely a "C-," based on the Crawfords' financial support to the school, but that was another matter.

"Yes, I most certainly can," said Combs with as much southern charm as he could stomach. However, Mr. Crawford, the information David provides could help the investigation in terms of where others were at the time of the accident," said Combs attempting to downplay the crime and draw blame away from David.

This seemed to appease Crawford Sr. for the moment. The conversation was again interrupted by the relentless ringing of a telephone before Crawford Sr. reluctantly stepped away. Combs jumped at the opportunity to press David about his relationship with Tessa and, caught off guard, David's face flushed red and his hands trembled when he revealed that he "liked her a lot; they all did." David also said he and two other boys were near the tracks shooting pellet guns and "just messing around," the day Tessa was killed.

"Thank you, David, you've been very helpful and I'm going to look for you at the next Trojan's game," said Combs with an arm around David's shoulder and a reassuring squeeze. Combs was confident David knew more than he was willing to tell. If only he could gather enough evidence to bring him in.

ELEVEN

Brandon woke to angry voices carried into the attic through the floor vent as he lay on a thin mattress inside the three-story Victorian. He was just nine years old when he came to live with Aunt Katrina after his mother died of heart failure. No one ever talked about his father, whose most current address was a P.O. Box in Belle Glade, FL. Brandon never even thought about him. A classic dead-beat, they were better off without him. Aunt K had her own problems which involved a long history of stellar boyfriends and substance abuse. She was a human magnet for the man-child desperate for a mommy figure. None of them had jobs or cars and no sooner did she meet the squatters they would settle in and begin barking orders. She treated Brandon like a big brother even though she was twenty years his junior, relying on him whenever the flavor of the month became jealous, angry or worse. There was always a new one and all of them were good-for-nothing leeches.

Memories of his mother were good but fading with each passing year. At seven years old he sat on her lap turning the steering wheel while she worked the peddles as they drove through town. Weekends were sometimes spent in the park. She read mysteries and he played ball and climbed the Angel Oaks that lined the length of Battery Park. They challenged each other with who could blow the biggest bubble or make the scariest face which always resulted in a fit of giggles. He decided to take up swearing once but stopped after a memorable encounter with a bar of Palmolive. They had little money, but somehow, she managed to buy art supplies which they used to decorate brown grocery bags displayed on the refrigerator. She recognized his talent early on and encouraged him to keep at it. When she died, he began spending time at the tracks and it was there he took his craft to the next level producing the first of many murals that covered the boxcars.

Reaching for his jacket, he turned onto his side and pulled it tight covering his ear. Light peered through holes near the window where parts of the roof and ceiling had deteriorated. Water damage throughout the attic resulted in large brown clouds over frayed drywall. There was no lock on the bedroom door, so Brandon kept a small lamp on a cardboard box lit throughout the night.

That evening the party in the old Victorian began at nine o'clock and continued until dawn. Brandon left the basketball courts shortly after the party started and found a house filled with people when he returned. The walls vibrated as deep bass and a distinct musky scent permeated the dilapidated structure while thick cigarettes passed from one hand to another. Inching his way through the crowd, he was nearly to the stairwell when he saw her in the hallway.

Fitz Callaway, number seven that year, was dressed in jeans and a wife-beater two sizes too small. An unemployed security guard, he spent most of his time lifting weights and sucking in his cheeks while flexing in the bathroom mirror. He towered over her with tight fists as they argued. Hidden in the dark stairwell, Brandon watched and waited. Fitz moved in closer as Aunt K leaned into the wall with arms folded. A menacing face with bulging eyes shouted while she glared at him in silence. Whatever it was that made him mad, he had no business treating her that way. This new one was a monster of a man with the smallest part of him likely the empty space between his ears. Brandon stood ready to intervene, and when he pushed her back against the wall for the second time, he was on his feet. He stood behind the giant contemplating if he should bash his skull with something heavy, but there was no weapon in sight, and if there were, it would most likely be used against him.

"Leave her alone," he said squarely into massive shoulder blades covered in circular wisps of hair.

Hearing the small voice, Fitz turned slowly perusing the teenager with an arrogant smirk.

"Beat it, kid," he said unfazed while Aunt K stuck out her tongue at his back.

He picked up where he left off barking at her about whatever it was that had bruised his frail ego.

"Don't talk to her that way!" Brandon warned with raised fists.

"We is conversating! Now, what did I tell you?"

Fitz's idea of a conversation resembled that of a sergeant on day one of boot camp. The veins in his thick neck popped as angry blood rushed to the stump on his shoulders. He spoke through clenched teeth while jabbing a finger into Brandon's chest just below the Adam's Apple. Fitz, not the sharpest tool in the shed, had the insecurity of a small man, a hair trigger temper and a limited intellectual capacity. All that rolled up into one winner, winner, chicken dinner! Whatever she saw in him was a mystery. The angrier he got, the more his skin glistened with sweat as his body worked to cool this hot headed neanderthal.

"I said, you leave her alone!" shouted Brandon with more authority than he knew he had in him.

His heart raced and his legs turned to rubber, but still, he couldn't allow the loser meathead to have his way. Afterall, Aunt K was counting on him to take care of things. She was his mother's little sister, and she looked exactly like her, having the same wide smile, oval eyes and quirky giggle. If he didn't intervene, Fitz would think he could boss them around and Brandon wasn't having any of it.

Fitz, more than a foot taller than Brandon was three times his weight. The demanding voice behind him only added to his already volatile temperament and this time, he meant business. In a flash he sent Brandon sailing into the wall where he landed in a heap. Aunt K, blocked by the bully's wide frame, went berserk.

"Stop it!" she screamed as the WWF smackdown ensued with the duo throwing punches and banging into walls. A strike, intended for Brandon's face, resulted in a gaping hole in the drywall and bloodied fist. Fitz cradled his injured hand for only a moment before grabbing Brandon by the collar and pinning him against the wall. The brawl, however, was short lived as Brandon had had enough of the overgrown imbecile. Sweat poured from his face as he struggled to free himself from the bully's tight grip. If he didn't think fast, he'd end up with a battered face, and broken teeth. He knew he couldn't keep fighting him and survive, so with every ounce of strength he had, he lunged with a swift right knee to the groin. Bugling eyes turned to shock, then fear as Fitz melted onto the floor and curled into a fetal position. The bruiser was hurt good and deserved everything he got. He rolled into a tight ball and let out an annoying high-pitched moan.

"That'll teach you mess with us! Big sissy baby!"

"Look at him, Aunt K! He ain't so tough now!" shouted Brandon.

Fitz rolled from one side to the other clutching his knees and then the unthinkable. The bruiser started to cry. The tearless wail, loud and ridiculous was a pitiful sympathy plea for the benefit of Aunt K. Brandon thought a good kick to the ribs might shut him up, but as he cocked his leg back, he was pulled from behind by long thin arms that grabbed his waist. Aunt K, worried what would happen when Fitz recovered, begged him to leave for his own good.

"Go! Get out now! Before he back up. You go!" she commanded.

"But you be all alone," he protested while keeping one eye on the wailing lump.

"I'll be ok. Go, now!" she demanded as she pushed him toward the door. It was the right thing to do, and he knew it. When the bully was back on his feet, he'd come looking for Brandon and that would be the end of him. He hurried out of the house even though he had nowhere to go.

Brandon walked with his backpack through downtown Tennison Park past Jay's Laundromat which was dark inside. He headed east several more blocks to the only other place he knew he'd have a roof over his head. Crawling inside the open boxcar, he lay on the damp floor far enough inside so as not to be seen. He propped his jacket underneath his head and thought about his mother as angry tears filled his eyes.

Twelve

Combs had had his fill of rich white kids, but knew he had to remain unbiased. He focused on suspect number two, a young boy from Tennison Park with a record of petty theft seen running from the woods minutes after Tessa was killed.

Combs parked several houses from the old Victorian and sat watching the house while three men exited quickly. He waited for a pause in activity before shutting the door of the gray Chevy Impala and making his way over broken concrete towards the only known address for Brandon Michael Thompson.

The old Victorian must have been beautiful at one time, but now it was in severe disrepair with several boarded windows and traces of yellowish paint that remained on mostly gray slats. On the wide porch, lay a striped Tabby curled up inside the sunken cushion of an exhausted old couch. The cat gave a wide yawn and stretched its long body when Combs appeared. It turned onto its back pushing its chin upward with hind legs fully extended. Combs gave the Tabby a quick belly scratch before he knocked three times on the rickety screen door.

"Nobody home," a raspy voice shouted from inside the house.

Combs knocked one more time and then opened the door and stepped inside reaching back to unsnap the clasp on his revolver, keeping his hand near it.

"Detective Combs, Charleston Police Department ma'am, can I have a word with you"?

The wood floors were sticky under his shoes and the house was trashed. Beer bottles and Styrofoam cups lay strewn about. Furniture was damaged or severely worn and window treatments were ripped or missing. The smell of cigarettes and stale booze was nauseating. Combs walked cautiously though the house carefully stepping over debris and garbage hoping he wouldn't have to call in C.P.S. He continued through what could be considered a dining room past a filthy bathroom with a sink filled to the brim with yellowish liquid and noticed a hypodermic needle near the faucet.

"Detective Combs with Charleston Police Department; show yourself, I'm coming in," shouted Combs pulling out his .38 and pointing it upward.

The house was silent and then a small cough and a moan were heard from a room on the right at the end of a hallway. Combs stood to the side of the doorway with both hands on the gun and cautiously peered through the open doorway. Katrina lay partially dressed on a bare mattress, her eyes rolling upward. Next to her, a giant of a man with thick arms and legs stared straight ahead motionless.

Combs watched as paramedics lifted Katrina onto the stretcher while the coroner went to work. He searched through the rest of the house along with two C.P.D. officers and found a mostly empty attic except for a secret compartment camouflaged in a corner of stained drywall. The drywall, which had been purposely cut and carefully reset contained a worn picture of a young black woman with a small Caucasian boy, a pack of Marlboro cigarettes and two cans of Orr-Lac spray paint. Combs gathered the materials in plastic bags, finished his business and started to make his way back to the Chevy when he noticed a young boy walking cautiously towards the house. The boy spotted Combs, turned around and began to run. Combs, grateful he had quit smoking years ago, gave chase. He finally caught up with the boy several blocks from the home when he tripped on a curb and tumbled to the ground.

Brandon spent the night at C.P.D. giving Combs enough time to do more research. Resolute and defiant, he sat with arms tight across his chest in a small dimly lit room at C.P.D. His clothes were wrinkled, dirty and badly worn. Traces of yellow and blue paint and a caricature of a mouse with an obscene gesture covered the front of his t-shirt. Combs stared through the glass studying Brandon for several minutes before entering the room.

"You know this girl, Brandon?" said Combs laying photographs of Tessa on the table one by one directly in front of him.

"No," said Brandon shaking his head and wincing at the gruesome photos of the dead girl.

"Ever see her on the street?" said Combs.

"I ain't seen, her none," said Brandon shaking his head.

"You play basketball with her father at Tennison Park?" Combs said raising his voice.

"No."

"Why you lying to me, Brandon? I know you recognize her... pretty girl like that's sort of hard to forget, don't you think?"

"She all right. But I don't know her."

"You're lying! You saw her at Tennison Park courts!"

"You played basketball while she watched, isn't that right?" shouted Combs.

"But I don't know her!"

"Why'd you run!"

"I done know."

"Did you touch her, Brandon?"

"No, I didn't touch her!"

"Did you kill her!"

"NO!"

"Why'd you run?!" shouted Combs.

"I don't know," he said as tears filled his eyes spilling down his cheeks.

"Tell me about that," yelled Combs, pushing further.

The boy was scared, and it didn't take long to break him. Most of the suspects he encountered were hard core and didn't come close to caving this easy.

Combs listened intently while Brandon detailed how he came to live with Aunt K, the events at the Victorian, the fight and the time he spent at the tracks. Combs was silent as he listened to the boy for nearly an hour before gathering the evidence and leaving the room. Tessa was found just 50 feet from the boxcar where Brandon slept that night, and he had no alibi the day she was killed. Could the boy have committed this crime? He was desperate to get enough evidence for a conviction, but his gut said no, her killer was not Brandon Thompson.

The wipers squeaked across a cracked windshield tossing heavy rain from one side of the window to the other. The street was lined with one mansion more beautiful than the next and Combs felt the anger rise inside of him. Not long ago, these mansions had been tended to by slaves and the number one suspect, Brandon Thompson was up against a community of racists itching to seal the conviction. Combs was desperate to find solid evidence that would direct the investigation elsewhere. He passed the house and then stopped suddenly squealing to a halt on the quiet tree lined street. He backed up too quickly nearly missing a vehicle to the left that let out an angry rebuttal. The old Impala had seen better days, but Combs still liked the way it drove and the power of the V8 engine. It was a trusted beast with good bones and lots of room.

Combs hated talking with families that had lost or missing loved ones. The awkward silence and his lack of sympathetic social graces frustrated him as well as those he spoke with. He pulled into the Rhodes' driveway and sighed giving himself some time to put on his game face.

He rang the doorbell and waited and was about to pound the door knocker but stopped as he heard the click of a deadbolt. Somehow Mr. Rhodes looked much older than he had had several weeks ago. The crevices under his eyes were deeper and his gait seemed slow and without purpose. His clothes were wrinkled and worn and looked like they had been slept in for days. His once shiny black hair was grayer and the white nubs on his chin were well overgrown giving the appearance of a homeless vagabond. The well-kept Tudor was quiet and pristine, but there wasn't a single light on which made the beautiful home dark and spooky. Mr. Rhodes was always gracious and welcoming even though it was clear he was falling apart. Combs followed Rhodes to the back of the house and noticed Mrs. Rhodes standing in a bedroom doorway, still and quiet, gazing straight ahead as they walked past her invisible. Completely silent, she was in another world and the eerie encounter had Combs on edge. The death of Tessa had indeed taken its toll the likes of which Combs had seen many times before. However, Combs felt it was his duty to see his customers face to face. A phone call would have been much easier, but Combs considered it disrespectful even though he loathed the task.

Rhodes offered Combs a beverage, coffee, tea, water... scotch?

They sat in the sunroom just off the formal living room in silence drinking Scotch in view of the Wild Dunes Golf Course that bordered the Rhodes' property. Not wanting to push him just yet, Combs glanced at Rhodes and waited as drops of rain trickled down beveled glass windows of the octagon enclosure. Finally, he spoke.

"I just can't get my arms around it, you know," said Rhodes more to himself than Combs while he swirled the ice in his glass repeatedly.

"She... she was just here a minute ago, he said with one outstretched palm. And then... and then, she was gone," said Rhodes lowering his head to his chest.

Combs felt sick to his stomach, the same way he always felt when he had to endure these kinds of conversations.

"We'll find him. We're getting closer, but we're not there yet. I need more. Please, please, Mr. Rhodes, if there's anything, anything at all, that you think might help."

Rhodes was silent for what seemed like an eternity staring into his glass and then quite suddenly he lifted his head.

"Yes, yes, there is something," he said nodding slowly.

"I don't know, but maybe. Maybe it's something, I don't know," said Rhodes, his voice trailing off as he stared out into the backyard.

"What, what?" said Combs.

"What is it, Mr. Rhodes?"

"Those!" said Rhodes lifting his long arm straight ahead and pointing to the backyard.

"Those what?" said Combs, urgently scanning the backyard and rolling green mounds in the golf course.

"Those! The roses," said Rhodes with an eerie half smile.

"She got lots and lots of those. They were always left on the front steps, but we never knew who sent them," said Rhodes turning to look directly at Combs with wide, desperate eyes.

Bingo thought Combs. It wasn't so much the roses as it was the gut feeling that told him there was something here.

BRANDON WALKED the tracks carrying a tattered backpack while Aunt Katrina lay unconscious at Roper Hospital of Charleston. He wondered if he would see her alive again. The cop had scared him, and he wanted to tell her about it, but she wouldn't even open her eyes. She had a plastic cup over her mouth, and something hooked up to her arm. The room was sterile and quiet except for the nursing staff that moved in and out of the room checking instruments and writing on clipboards. She looked frail and small in the hospital bed, and he wanted to stay with her but visiting hours were over. He hadn't eaten in twenty-four hours, and he was hungry, so he took the sandwich wrapped in plastic from her tray and stuffed it in his coat pocket. He had the old Victorian to himself now that the meathead was gone, but it was lonely, so he headed to the tracks to do what he loved.

The boxcars on each side of the small path kept him safely hidden from view. He pulled at the brim of a shrunken t-shirt that periodically crept past broken beltloops to his waist. Stopping in front of his mural, he saw black paint from someone with the initials DC that said he was an artist. No one except Barbara had ever told him he was good at anything. Brandon reached inside his jacket to retrieve the spray cans hidden inside the lining. He found an unmarked boxcar with wide panels and began. This one was unlike all the others. He had never done a portrait before, and he wasn't sure if he could remember exactly what she looked like. It had been nearly eight years since Barbara died and with each passing year, he felt he was losing more of her. He scanned the area, darting between boxcars carefully to be sure no one was around. He stayed close enough to the trees so he could easily make a run for it if he needed to. Not that any of the FRA could truly catch him. Most of the them were heavy smokers, overweight and barely able to walk let alone chase a tagger with the speed of a gazelle. On a good day, their tar filled lungs could barely get them up a short flight of stairs. Brandon was lean and fast, and he knew the terrain well. The nearest station was nearly twenty cars south and he picked a boxcar that gave him a clear view all the way down the line. If the rail authority were to come around, he could spot them before they noticed him. It was nearly dinner time and Brandon surmised the plump FRA that patrolled the tracks were spilling over the tops of bar stools in greasy spoons where they would dine for no less than three hours on taxpayer dollars. After years of tagging, Brandon knew when it was safe. He dug into a pile of discarded wood and pulled out a tall, sturdy pallet, propping it against the car's wall to use as stairs to climb the side. He began with a heart shaped face followed by oval eyes with thin brows that stretched from the bridge of the nose just past the outer eye. He sprayed black paint into his left palm and dabbed at it with a thin brush that he used to create fine lashes to frame the eyes. The cheekbones were high with a dab of light-colored paint just above the ridge. The lips were full, and the smile was kind. Loose curls flowed down one side of her face to just below the jaw with one short strand hovering near an eye. The dimple on the left cheek was subtle, and the tiny scar above the right eyebrow was placed where the man, who they said was his father, had struck her. The scar had healed into a faint jagged line barely noticeable except for the residue of cautiousness that surfaced in the company of strangers. A tiny dab of white in each eye produced the sparks that brought her to life. The mural was finished, and it was as though Barbara was alive again.

Thirteen

I watched as the crowd entered the theater and felt the sweat begin to gather on my back and neck, my palms damp with perspiration. This was my first time leading a team in a mock trial in front of one hundred and twenty Harvard law students and faculty and I was terrified.

Students with the highest scores were chosen and divided into two teams, defense and prosecution. I would lead the defense. My opponent was the son of James Klein of Klein, Brown, LLC. Klein, Brown were well known throughout the northeast having won several high-profile criminal cases involving a handful of celebrities and high net worth individuals. James Jr. was a humble and studious fellow, but when it came to competition, he was fierce and relentless.

The case involved the death of a young woman and accusation against her longtime boyfriend. I prepared hard for this day reassuring myself that my team's due diligence was solid, but inside I was filled with fear. Leah sat in the front row off to the right and smiled whenever I glanced her way, compounding my anxiety even more.

Students continued to pile in until finally every seat was filled. Several latecomers were forced to stand at the back and along the aisles of the large theater. The rumble of conversation provided only a mild distraction from the tension that was building inside of me. The overhead lights appeared brighter than normal and the room grew warmer by the minute.

I spotted Professor John Taylor, head of legal as he entered the theater and began his descent to the front of the room. He was repeatedly interrupted by students eager for his attention. Several of them made their way from across the room to talk to John which really slowed things down. Taylor was a legend of sorts on, and off campus having won a particularly high-profile case in 1957 when he had his own firm. The case resulted in the acquittal of a beloved CEO of a large local corporation. At the time, the company employed a good majority of the households in Cambridge and if convicted, the community was at high risk of economic disaster. The people in Cambridge were grateful and they never forgot it.

John was flawless in the courtroom and just as talented in the classroom. He knew every one of his students by name and pushed them to the brink and then rewarded their efforts with generous accolades. They respected him and when they left Harvard, they were handpicked by the best firms in the country.

Taylor gave me a quick nod of support the way he always did when he had special affinity for a student. I was chosen to lead the team because John wanted my courtroom skill equal to what I had mastered in the classroom. I always knew this would be the hardest part.

The jury took their seats in a box off to the right. Five male and seven female students chatted as the doors to the theater were closed and the room quieted. John Taylor, acting as judge, took his seat at a desk in the front of the room and began reviewing documents. After several minutes, he pounded a gavel four times and stood as the room quieted.

"All rise," said John. He walked to the front of the theater and stopped in the center.

"Ladies and gentlemen. Before we begin, let me remind all of you that today's session will be run as if it were an actual court of law. You will abide by the rules and courtesies in a courtroom," said John as he scanned the room.

"For those who may wish to challenge with reckless commentary or other interruption, you will be asked to leave, and your absence duly noted. No excuses, no exceptions. Let's begin. You may be seated."

John Taylor provided the group with an overview of the case and the charges levied against the defendant, Joshua Auerbach. He introduced the two teams and asked each of us to stand as he identified us by name.

James Klein, Jr., leading the prosecution, had steel blue eyes, chiseled features and a thick head of sandy hair perfectly set with some sort of glue-like substance. The cemented hair, well suited for a parachute jump or F5 hurricane, was a bit much for a mock trial. He stood eagerly waiting to address the crowd in a tweed suit and cobalt tie which coincidently matched his eyes. His sleeves were rolled halfway to his elbows revealing a thick gold watch worth more than my Datsun. If his due diligence was anywhere close to his physical preparation, I was in deep trouble. I noted females in the jury take a liking to him right out of the gate and felt instantly intimidated in my worn suit with blown out pockets.

Klein delivered a compelling opening statement slamming the defendant with harsh accusations.

"Not only did Kelly suffer at the hands of Joshua that night; she suffered throughout their entire ten-year relationship. Think about that, ten whole years," Klein said solemnly to a quiet audience that hung on every word.

"Ladies and gentlemen, I intend to prove that Kelly fled the apartment that night in fear for her life," said James. He paced confidently across the room speaking clear and dramatic accusations to an attentive jury for eighteen minutes and 45 seconds. James had them spellbound. He could have done quite well in the theater program I surmised, but unfortunately for me, he chose law.

"Kelly's injuries, folks, were NOT consistent with a fall. These injuries," he said, pointing to a female torso propped on an easel, "are the result of abusive acts. Abuse by a jealous and angry young man desperate to hold on to a dying relationship," said James.

Klein continued pounding the jury with slanderous statements in rapid succession, pausing to look directly at the defendant with an ominous glare. As quickly as he spoke, I wrote. I couldn't afford to miss a single point. When he finished, I would be ready with a solid rebuttal overturing every shred of doubt in the minds of the jury.

Finally, the male model finished, and the court adjourned. I had drunk nearly a pitcher of water while Klein strolled the catwalk and I felt I would bust wide open at any moment. I had only ten minutes before the group would return to the theater and I had to think fast. I grabbed my notes and ran toward the nearest latrine while rehearsing the rebuttal in my head. I sensed a high degree of empathy from the females in the jury and I had to find a way to sway them. Finally, in front of the urinal I found relief, but before I could finish, the door flung open and in walked Klein and the rest of the Calvin Klein crew.

"Campbell, you're gonna choke," shouted Rob Donaldson, the prosecution's second in command and most obnoxious one in the group. He walked past me and slapped my back in jest pushing me forward as I was about to hit the flush lever. My hand, hit the lever and at the same time, caught the edge of my notepad, sending it straight into the urinal and under a deluge of water. Everything I had written down for the last half hour was now in a swirl of blue ink headed straight for the sewer. I grabbed at the soaked pad brushing off the water and blotting it with paper towels, but it was no use, my notes were a blur of soggy, unrecognizable blue ink. I was devastated and could only stare in horror as my career flowed down the drain in an instant.

"Sorry, Campbell, said the moron with minimal sincerity as he looked at me in horror, mouth agape.

I walked back to the theater in a state of shock and took my seat and could only stare straight ahead while the crowd slowly filed back into the theater.

The only sound was that of my heels echoing as I made my way to the front of the room for opening statement. My necktie was suddenly too tight, and my jacket felt heavy and suffocating. My shirt, thick with perspiration, stuck to my skin like a thick coat of paint. I cleared my throat several times, but there was no sound. My voice had all but vanished. I turned to address the audience and the blood drained from my face. I froze. I watched as they looked to one another in bewilderment, but still, I couldn't speak.

"Mr. Campbell?" said John Taylor.

The faint hum of a fan echoed throughout the theater and someone at the back of the room sneezed. I knew the opening remarks were crucial to winning the case. A strong start would have a marked influence on the jury as some jurors would undoubtedly make up their minds early on.

"Mr. Campbell?" said John again with more urgency.

I wiped the sweat from my brow with a handkerchief and stuffed it in the pocket of my trousers hoping it wouldn't fall through the hole in my pocket and onto the floor. Another minute passed before I was finally able to find my voice.

"Ladies and gentlemen," I began more quietly than I had intended.

"Mr. Campbell," said John, with some impatience, you will need to speak up, please so all of the room can hear you."

I looked over my shoulder at John who gave a nod and quick reassuring smile. I took a deep breath, letting the air fill my lungs completely and exhaled slowly feeling some of the tension leave my body. I began again, this time more loudly pushing myself to remain focused and on point. I moved to stand next to Joshua Auerbach and rested my hand lightly on his shoulder and began to tell his story.

"Ladies and gentlemen, what we have here is a man. A man who loved," I said with unintentional vulnerability. It was right then that I thought of Tessa. Her freckles, the shy way she laughed, how she made friends with just about everyone, and how my heart still cared for her.

"This is the story of a man who loved for a lifetime and is now devastated with grief."

My words were passionate and the sorrow I described was my own. I took them through the quarrel and how Kelly darted from the dorm room that night alone and then the tragic fall. Joshua wasn't there to protect Kelly that night just as I wasn't there to protect Tessa Rhodes when she was murdered. Halfway through my remarks I stood in front of the jury making eye contact with each one speaking to them individually. The more I spoke, the more confident I became, the entire room hanging on every word. The jury followed my movements across the room while I took them methodically through that night including the fight, the accident and a love they shared for nearly a lifetime. I moved to stand near the defendant and told the story of a friendship that evolved into a romance that continued for years right up to that terrible night, the tragic end.

"Does this, ladies and gentlemen, sound like a dying relationship? I don't think so," I said.

The jury was somber, and I knew I had them right where I wanted them. When I finished, the utter silence in the large theater told me I had accomplished what I had set out to do.

We adjourned for an hour lunch and soon after we returned, the jury foreman stood and read the verdict.

"Does the jury foreman have the verdict?" said John.

"Yes, we do."

"What did the jury decide?" said John.

"Not guilty!"

The theater erupted.

"Congratulations," said John.

To my surprise, the entire theater applauded. I could hardly believe it. I took off my jacket and turned around to a standing ovation while John Taylor made his way over to our table.

We celebrated that night in a small Irish pub in Harvard Square till dawn. The noisy bar, packed wall to wall with Harvard law students and faculty, buzzed with the excitement of the trial. Commentary from both sides of the argument could be heard from every corner of the room. We reveled in our victory in the center of the long bar with puffed chests and our heads held high. Half a dozen shot glasses lined the bar as kudos to our victory.

We drank one honorary shot with John Taylor and then another honorary shot because we drank with John Taylor. Every excuse for another shot sounded better than the one before it. That's pretty much how the rest of the night went. The bar was packed to the brim and the future lawyers of America were feeling no pain. As the clock neared 4:00am, the jukebox blared, Don McLean's "American Pie" and like drunken sailors, we sang out loud arm in arm till they turned on the lights and kicked us out. I had stopped counting the number of shots I drank. They went down so easy. It was the best night of my life and then it quickly became the worst night of my life.

I stumbled down the path to Wigglesworth and into the dorm bouncing from wall to wall as I made my way through the building to the small apartment. I fumbled for my key and dropped it somewhere underneath me while talking to myself. I had a lot to say, but no one was listening, so I thought. After searching on my hands and knees for several minutes, I finally found the key inside my pocket and swore while I wrestled with the key in the lock. Someone from down the hall shouted.

"Shut up, you jerk," said a raspy voice followed by the rapid slam of a door.

"Have a nice nit," I shouted back to the door slammer.

Another door opened and a burly guy with tousled hair appeared wearing boxers covered in sailboats.

"Do you need some help," he said with a threatening scowl.

"Noooooo," I said swaying. I've got ever-thin under control.

"I'm jist a little seasick," I said with a chuckle hoping the big guy would appreciate my humor.

He didn't. He continued to stand in the hallway watching me.

"Get your sorry butt inside before I knock you out," he said.

With a sloppy salute, I said "goodnight" and turned as fast as I could toward the door. With a bit of luck, I pushed the key into the lock and scrambled inside.

"Ga-night everybody," I shouted at the closed door.

It was just about then everything began to go saucy. I felt it in my stomach. Something wasn't right. Then, the room began to spin, and I noticed the air smelled of dirty socks and Fritos. I tried to deny it, but there was no use, I was going to be sick. I made a run for it and just as I opened the latrine door, yellow liquid shot from my mouth like a fire hose in full throttle. I missed the toilet, splashing vomit all over the tiled floor emptying everything I had for the next three hours.

Exhausted and delirious, I stood up and reached for a towel. Stepping into the slippery liquid, I lost my footing and slid towards the basin and then away from it, desperately grasping for the towel and then ripping the holder out of the wall. I fell backward and then all at once, I was in the air and just as quickly on the floor as my head slammed on the ceramic tile.

When I woke, the sun was beating down on my face through the small window above the shower. I heard a moan and smelled vomit as I lay there. I was alive but I couldn't move. The pounding in my head was in sync with my throbbing back, and I could hardly breathe. It took another hour before

I was able to pull myself upright. I was a mess. I sat on the floor with my head propped against my knees in agony. I felt sorry for myself and spent the next two days in bed.

Word spread throughout Harvard of my courtroom victory and suddenly, I had more friends than I knew what to do with. It seemed everyone knew my name. "Hey Des," said a chubby kid in a thick crochet sweater as he passed me in the hall. I didn't know him, but he knew me. "Would you sign my yearbook"? said a petite girl with long straight bangs and dark eyes. "Sure," I said, tucking my books under my arm while I wrote a scribbled note on the corner of a page. Girls seemed to notice me now too. They watched me as I made my way through the cafeteria to the main corridor. I wasn't quite comfortable with this newfound celebrity at first. But then, I began to like it. Too much.

I was invited to several high-profile parties hosted by Harvard board members and notable alumni and my confidence soared. For the first time, I felt important. I received inquiry letters from several well-known firms and with graduation just weeks away, I was riding high.

It was a Friday night black tie event in Mount Auburn, one of the most exclusive neighborhoods in Cambridge. The ornate row of homes was elevated on a small hill just past Mount Auburn Cemetery.

"Good evening, sir," said the valet parker.

I scanned the area before I realized he was talking to me and then handed over my keys. Adjusting the jacket of my rented tuxedo, I patted my hair down with both hands before stopping to admire the beautiful three-story estate. The house was lit up top to bottom and from the driveway I could hear a rumble of conversation coming from inside the home. I walked up several rows of steps to the main entrance where an older man I assumed was a butler welcomed me inside directing me to a room down the hall.

"Welcome to Kempsford house," said the lumpy man with droopy cheeks.

I walked past a grand split stairway with walls decorated in oil painted portraits. Interesting glass sculptures sat illuminated on small tables in the main foyer and the walls in the hallway were adorned with large black and white photographs. A woman in a red leather dress and matching heels brushed against me on her way to the lavatory. "Pardon me," she said with a wide smile and the most perfect set of teeth I had ever seen. Her sandy blonde hair was set in a Brigitte Bardot up-do, and as I turned the corner, a row of eyes followed her as she made her way down the hall.

Just as I was about to enter the parlor, the very last photograph caught my eye. The resemblance was remarkable. She had long straight blonde hair and light eyes. Her cheekbones were set high and tiny freckles sprinkled her nose and cheeks. If I didn't know better, I would have said it was Tessa Rhodes. My heart beat faster, and as I studied the familiar face, a flood of memories surfaced. I began scouring the hallway for more photographs of her, but John Taylor motioned for me to join him in a group of four- or five-party goers.

"This is Desmond Campbell, everyone. He's going to be one of the best criminal defense lawyers in the country," he beamed with an arm on my shoulder.

I was introduced to two judges, several partners and the owner of the home, Martin Kempsford. Martin was a member of Harvard's Board of Directors and the father of the girl that resembled Tessa Rhodes. Martin showed a keen interest in me right from the get-go. He fired a barrage of questions and listened intently as I spoke.

"I'd like to work in human rights. That's what stirs me up," I said trying to sound more confident than I really was.

"Honorable," said Martin with dressed up sincerity.

He had a hand on my back as he introduced me to another partner in the firm they headed. Both Martin and the other guy stuck to me like glue.

"We're always looking for talent such as yours, Desmond and we can offer you more security than a career in human rights," he said without a hint of guilt.

I was on my third Guinness when he introduced me to his daughter, Joanna, the girl that looked like Tessa Rhodes. Joanna Kempsford was a knockout and more beautiful in person than the photographs. She held out her hand palm down and I shook it awkwardly, not realizing she was expecting me to kiss it. She frowned but only for a second.

"Nice to meet you, Desmond, I'm Joanna Kempsford" she said with confident sophistication.

She offered to show me around the house, and I followed her into the main foyer like a sheep to the slaughter. Joanna wore an off the shoulder dress that displayed the curves of her waist and hips perfectly. The back was cut low revealing the base of her back and I followed her through the house in a daze, ignorant to much of what she said.

"The house was built in the 1800's and was a strategy post for Union officials just prior to the Civil War," she said with pride. She sauntered through three floors of the house relaying interesting facts and dates effortlessly. It was evident she had done the tour guide gig before. She was good at it.

"Much of the pre-Civil War furniture has remained in the house," she said referencing a small antique desk.

"Ulysses Grant sat right there at that desk. My father likes everyone to know," she mused with an eye roll.

Joanna finished the tour and seemed glad to be done with it and was now on a mission to liven things up.

"Come with me!" she commanded with mischievous excitement while taking hold of my hand. Apparently, she had run out of fun facts and the history lesson was over. She led me through the kitchen, down a hallway and then to a spiral staircase and into the basement's wine cellar. She flicked on lights in the cave like structure that illuminated rows and rows of bottles nestled in tall wooden shelves. Near the back wall, a crystal chandelier hung over a small sitting area with leather chairs, a small couch and a coffee table made from a barrel.

"Look at them all!" she exclaimed, running her hands seductively over the bottles.

"Isn't it wonderful?" she said leaning back against rows of bottles in that five-alarm dress.

"It sure is," I said unsure of exactly which wonderful we were talking about.

In the cellar she again took hold of my hand and led me through the long room stopping at the very last row of shelves filled with Scotch Whiskey.

"You have to try this one," she said with determination.

She reached for one of the bottles and set it on the small table.

"This is one of the rarest and most expensive Scotch Whiskeys ever made. It's a 1940 Macallan," she said with overdone seriousness and the assumption I would recognize the bottle's value.

"Would you like to try some?" she said.

"Sure, I'm not fussy," I said.

Oblivious to the lifestyles of the rich and famous, at that point, I would have drunk just about anything she put in front of me.

She opened the bottle without hesitation and poured it into two etched tumblers. She handed me a glass and raised hers, "Cheers," she said with seductive eyes that undressed me without a fight.

The whiskey tasted good. Very good. We sipped the Scotch and then another and talked all about me well into midnight. Before I knew it, she was sitting close. So close, I could feel her breath on my cheek. Her perfume, a faint bouquet of spice and Jasmine, the red of her lips and the Scotch were all equally intoxicating.

"John Taylor speaks well of you. He said you're at the top of your class," said Joanna, as she reached for the lapel of my jacket.

She ran her palm up and down over the material in slow tender strokes as I envisioned hot steam shooting out both my ears.

"Yeah," I said nervously clearing my throat, hypnotized as my eyes followed her hand up and down my chest.

"John and I will be doing a lot of work together," I said trying my best to sound like a big shot.

My newfound notoriety, Joanna Kempsford and the whiskey had won the arm wrestle and I had lost. She stopped talking and studied me and then leaned forward kissing me lightly on my lips and then again more deeply. I kissed her back without hesitation before losing my marbles altogether. She moved to sit on my lap and held my face in both of her hands, kissing me on my lips, ear and then my neck and that's when it happened. It flew out of my mouth like a runaway Jet Train.

"Leah," I said in a low whisper of euphoric idiocy.

Joanna suddenly stopped and moved quickly from my lap to the couch. She reassembled her hair and dress in silence as I fumbled for something intelligent to say.

"Sorry" I said with a nervous cough.

"Leah is... well, she's my girlfriend," I said.

With a not-so-subtle yawn and wide stretch, I was on my feet in an instant. I checked my watch and Joanna, sensing defeat, stood with a frown. Straightening her dress again, she quickly rebounded.

"Shall we?" she said with a million-dollar smile.

Leading the way with her head held high, we left the cellar and reentered the party. I excused myself while Joanna skillfully immersed herself in a political conversation in full bloom.

"Don't be gone too long," she warned.

Apparently, she wasn't done with me just yet.

It was then I realized Joanna Kempsford had a specific motive. I turned around at just the right moment and witnessed a clandestine "thumbs up" from Joanna and a nod from Martin Kempsford who kept watch from across the room. It was now clear, Martin and Joanna worked as a team to lure new talent to the firm. I closed the bathroom door and stared at my reflection in the mirror.

"You're an idiot," I said out loud.

I quickly splashed cold water on my face and dabbed it with a towel before planning my escape. I opened the door a crack and waited till the coast was clear and then vanished through the main entrance and down the steps. I sped away from Kempsford House as fast as I could, and all I could think about was Leah and the jerk she fell in love with.

IT WAS three weeks since I saw Leah. She had called, but I was too busy being full of myself and then too ashamed of myself to answer the phone. I knew she was angry so like the coward I resembled, I avoided her altogether. As it turns out, she was angry – very angry, and I deserved everything I got.

I was already twenty minutes late to class when she confronted me in the center of Crimson Yard.

"Where have you been?" she said.

"I'm on my way to class, can we talk later?" I blurted and immediately regretted.

"No. We need to talk now!" she said nervously.

"Look, I know, we need to catch up," I said.

"Catch up? Catch up? she said.

"Are you kidding me!" she cried pushing my chest as books and papers loosed from my arm and fell to the ground.

"Leah, stop," I said.

"No, you stop!" she said.

"Stop being so fake! Who are you? I don't know who you are anymore Des," she said through teared eyes.

"I thought there was a 'we', but I don't see that anymore! There's just you," she said turning away and then back around.

"I can't do this anymore. I'm done, it's over!" she said.

I reached for her, but she quickly batted my hand away.

"Stay away from me. Don't you dare come near me!" she threatened.

I stood there like an idiot with my things all over the sidewalk and everyone watching.

Everyone except Leah... she was gone.

I FOUND an empty seat in the back of the lecture hall. The professor was scribbling something on the board as I settled in unnoticed. My mind was going a hundred miles an hour, and I couldn't concentrate, so I snuck out just as quickly as I had entered. Leah and I had never had a fight, not even an argument really, but the one we just had made up for it, and it was now crystal clear we were in serious trouble. She opened the apartment door with her coat on, and a suitcase told me she was going somewhere. Alone.

I thrust a bouquet of flowers at her and hoped for the best, but it had little influence.

"Where are you going?"

"I'm going away for a while. I'm done with exams, and I'm done with us," she said as my heart shattered into a million pieces.

"But can't we just talk?" I pleaded.

"No! I don't think you understand, I've been trying to talk to you for weeks" she said as she gathered her things.

"I've made up my mind. I'm going to Montana for a while. I need to think about what I want without you around," she said stoic.

Leah was right. I had been a pompous ass and I deserved everything I got. I made a feeble command in support of reconciliation knowing full well it would be shunned.

"No! You're not leaving until we work this out," I said.

"The cab is waiting. I have to go," she said unaffected as she said goodbye to a roommate that acknowledged me with a lingering death stare.

I walked her outside with my head hung low and helped her with the suitcase. The cab driver was in a hurry and since Leah had nothing to say, I simply kissed her on the cheek and told her I loved her.

She said she would call me when she got to Montana, but after two weeks, the call never came. I didn't know the aunt's name in Montana, so I headed over to Leah's old apartment to try and find out.

"What do *you* want?" said Bonnie Chen, the roommate that would have rather seen my toenails removed, doused in kerosene and lit on fire than offer Leah's whereabouts. She stood in the doorway wearing pajamas decorated in small rabbits and oversized slippers with bunny ears while she chomped on a celery stick loaded with peanut butter. Since Leah was gone, the gloves were off, and Bonnie had free reign to torture me unabated, something she had longed to do ever since her best friend fell in love with me. Unfortunately, I needed to be cordial, but only long enough to get the information I wanted. I would hold back the arsenal of insults I had stockpiled and release them as soon as it was safe to do so.

"I'm worried about Leah, and I need to reach her," I said, ignoring the sarcastic greeting and hoping the bags under my sad eyes would move Chen to extend a sympathy branch.

"She doesn't want to hear from *you*!" said Chen.

"She's moved on and you should too," she said with a smirk followed by a series of loud chomps.

"Haven't you done enough damage?" she said with one cocked eyebrow and peanut butter breath that made its way to me with the precision of a smart bomb.

"Leah is important to me, Bonnie!"

"I just need to talk to her and if she still doesn't want to see me, then I'll let it go," I lied.

Chen rearranged herself onto the other side of the doorway while contemplating my fate. I could see the wheels turning in her diabolical brain and I waited while trying my best to appear defeated.

"I'll give it to you on one condition," she said as the bunny ears bobbed in unison with her tapping foot.

"Ok, what's the condition," I said with joyless enthusiasm.

"I'll check with her first. If she doesn't want to talk to you, then you're not allowed to come over here and harass me again," she said as if our stimulating conversation were the highlight of my day.

"If she decides to talk to you, I'll leave the number under the door mat," she said.

"Check in a few days," she barked followed by a touching door slam that landed inches from my nose.

THE PHONE number was scribbled on a piece of paper the size of a gum wrapper. The chicken scratch was difficult to decipher which I surmised was purposeful. The rain didn't help as it made its way under the mat and onto the obscure penmanship of the savage that wrote it. I couldn't tell if the one's were sevens. the eights were threes, or the fours were nines as I examined the soggy mess like an FBI agent. I headed home and decided to jot down all the potential combinations and began making calls.

The first one was a beaut!

"Hello," said the person on the other end of the phone with a voice that sounded weak and ancient.

"Hello, this is Des, is Leah there?"

"Hello?" said the voice.

"Hello, this is Des, I'm looking for Leah," I said in a low shout.

Click.

There were two more hang ups, but on the fourth attempt, my voice had miraculously found its way to the clogged ear on the other end of the phone.

"Who?" she said.

"Des, my name is Des, and I'm looking for Leah," I urged.

"She's gone," she blurted.

"Gone?" I inquired.

"When will she be back?" I said hopeful.

"Never!" she barked.

"Gia's gone to Heaven not twenty years ago," she said with a cough.

"Are you a bill collector?" said the senior with faulty ears.

"If you are, go take a hike!" she barked like a pro before slamming the phone in my ear.

"No," I said to no one as I put the phone down and crossed that number off the list.

I had only three more phone numbers to go and if none of them belonged to Leah's aunt, I would have to visit the rabid bunny again and I wasn't looking forward to it.

The last number was a winner. Leah picked up the phone and sounded surprised to hear from me.

"How did you get this number?" she asked.

I wanted to tell her that I arm wrestled her evil ex-roommate and spent the past two days calling half of Montana, but I decided to play it cool.

"Chen gave it to me."

"Bonnie! She doesn't even like you!" she said.

"Really?" I said with the innocence of a newborn.

Leah and I talked for more than an hour. She let open the flood gates and said everything that was stored up inside for the past several weeks. She did most of the talking and I interjected the occasional apology which was the only smart thing out of my mouth since this whole mess started. She said she'd call me when she was ready, but her lack of enthusiasm was evident as we said goodbye and hung up.

Fourteen

Ray Combs stopped at a small coffee shop just a few feet near a purple-colored brick building which was the home of Page's Floristry. The smell of coffee and fresh bagels was somehow comforting. The coffee shop was clean and bright and there were interesting Victorian couches with an assortment of mismatch tables and chairs. The shop felt cozy, warm and inviting. Two counter girls with waist length hair and bright yellow smocks stood with their backs to Ray perusing photographs and giggling while he waited. He cleared his throat lightly and one of the girls turned.

"Can I help you?" said the waitress.

"A large black coffee please," said Ray.

Smiling to himself, he remembered how it was to be young and carefree. He envied them but wouldn't want to go back... not on your life. He was grateful the tough years were behind him and happy to be working at C.P.D. with a simple life that he cherished. Ray sipped his coffee and exited the shop, looking around at the well cared for businesses and manicured streets. Ornate lampposts were decorated with hanging flower baskets of every kind and color. Long strings of green vines fell from the baskets as they swayed gingerly in the morning breeze. Ray loved mornings, holding fast to the promise of the Lord's renewed forgiveness with each new day. He had encountered many people over the years desperately in need of forgiveness. Ray sipped his coffee and took a seat on a wood bench across from Page's so he could watch the shop before he went in to question the owner.

Donna Page stood in a corner of the shop putting the final touches on a large bouquet of yellow and purple Ranunculus that cascaded over a tall cylinder. Reading glasses rested nearly to the bottom of her nose as she carefully pulled at deep lavender organza ribbon, tying it exactly at the center of the vase. Her white collared shirt was tucked neatly into blue jeans that fit her petite figure perfectly. Donna's platinum blonde hair was tied in a short ponytail at the base of her neck and her silver hoop earrings shimmered in the early morning sunlight. She never took her hands off the ribbon when she greeted Ray with a warm and beautiful smile.

"Be with you in a minute," she said as she slid the holder down into the vase and carefully fastened the card inside the prongs of the floral pick.

Ray perused the shop while she worked, enjoying the variety of aromas that dominated every inch of the small floral shop with creaky wooden floors. The Temptations sang softly in the background filling the room with "I Got Sunshine," and Ray hummed to himself forgetting for a moment that he was on official business. He didn't know the names of the flowers except the easy ones.... roses, carnations, and orchids, but he liked them all and stopped several times to inspect the blooms that rested inside the earthy floral buckets.

Taking a step back, she smiled at her creation while she closed the window blind, protecting the delicate blooms from direct sunlight.

"And what can I do for you today?" she said warmly as she wiped her hands with a striped towel and swung it over her left shoulder.

"Hello," said Ray reaching out to shake Donna's hand.

He was suddenly aware of her attractiveness and could feel his face flush warm the way it always did when he met a beautiful woman. There was something indeed about Donna Page that he liked - something more than just pretty.

Donna was gracious, intelligent, and more than willing to help in whatever way she could. Donna revealed she was the late governor's daughter having grown up surrounded by dignitaries and all the prestige that went along with being the daughter of a high-ranking government official.

"I didn't much care for that kind of life," she said.

"I prefer to live a simple, quiet existence without all the attention and scrutiny that accompany being in the public eye."

"Nothing you do or say is ever really good enough no matter how well the intention," she said.

"My father wasn't the only one who bore the scars of public life."

"His job required that my siblings and I show the outside world how happy and well-adjusted we were. We suffered in silence for eight years while my father ran the state," she said.

"I don't miss those days at all."

"Well, enough about me, what can I help you with Mr. Combs?"

Ray was lost in Donna Page. Open, charming, and incredibly easy to talk to. He felt he had known her his whole life. Normally intimidated by the white, privileged Charleston society, he didn't feel that way with Donna Page, enjoying every moment of her company.

"I do remember a man that came in regularly to buy red roses," she said tapping a pencil softly on the tabletop.

"I haven't seen him for a few months and don't know his name, but I do recall he always paid in cash and didn't offer much in terms of conversation," she said with creased brow.

Ray showed Donna photographs of David Crawford, Jr., Brandon Thompson and several others, but Donna confirmed the man she saw was not any of them.

"No, he was much older," she said.

"None of those look familiar at all...I'm sorry."

Again, Ray had hit a wall, but inside he felt a giddy spark of something he hadn't felt in years. Her hand was warm and soft in his as he thanked her and said goodbye.

"You've been a great help. And....great company," he said as he reluctantly left the shop.

Fifteen

It rarely snowed at Christmas and in the still of night, thick snow rushed into the headlights before resting on the ground. The thrust of air woke the fallen snow, pushing it upward into a flurry of white behind me. I coasted quietly through the tree lined entrance and veered right, parking inside the circular driveway. Silencing the ignition, I sat for several minutes taking in the beauty of the old familiar mansion. The warm glow inside the home and lights along the garden walkways and perimeter illuminated tall pillars. A soft blanket of white rested over every inch of the property dimming rows of lanterns to a romantic hue. Just past the stable, an impressive buck lifted its head, its breath creating large puffs of steam that rose and quickly disappeared. It had been seven years since I was home, and a wave of apprehension washed over me.

I was just a boy full of insecurity and self-doubt when I left Charleston. I was different now, stronger and more confident. I felt instantly uneasy at Campbell mansion, but I didn't plan on staying long and if challenged, I was ready to face the demons that still lingered here.

I planned to meet with the local public defender. Leah had moved on and I couldn't blame her. She ignored my calls and then left Cambridge to spend the summer with an aunt in Montana, the visit apparently extended into the fall and now into Christmas. It was the happiest time of the year, but not for this unemployed and girlfriendless bundle of joy.

The icy snow crunched under my shoes as I made my way towards the old familiar dwelling. I stopped on the porch and peered into the side window. Jean was curled up on the couch sound asleep hugging a book. Next to her a fern nearly to the ceiling decorated in red bulbs and silver tinsel. She looked peaceful lying there waiting for me and I hated to wake her, but I had been driving for fifteen hours and I was tired and hungry.

IN THE morning, I woke to the familiar smell of coffee and biscuits and headed downstairs to investigate further. The mansion was as beautiful as ever. Jean, a consummate decorator had purchased a white rug that shown beautifully over black marble. Soft window treatments were gathered in mounds at the base of beveled glass windows. The mansion was meticulous, and I'd forgotten how stunning it was. Jean stirred a small saucer on the stovetop while Rudy sat at the bar reading the morning paper and sipping coffee from a large mug. They beamed with pride when I entered the kitchen, deliriously happy to have their son, the attorney, home at last. If I ended up staying in Charleston, I planned to look for a place of my own which would, no doubt, disappoint them, but that wasn't the worst of it. I would drop another bomb when I revealed I wouldn't be joining the firm. I finished breakfast and headed back upstairs to shower, eager to get into town for my secret meeting.

I PARKED behind Charleston's Legal Aid Bureau and made my way to the back entrance keeping my head low hoping to avoid any chance encounters with colleagues of Rudy. My meeting with the public defender was confidential, and I planned to keep it that way until after the meeting which had been arranged by John Taylor. John had become a trusted mentor and confidant over the years. John was the kind of father I had always longed for. As true as the day is long, John Taylor could always be counted on for support and rock-solid advice. John knew me well and never tried to dissuade me from a career in public service. He, too, was sympathetic to the poor and discriminated and was always supportive of my convictions.

"A good lawyer is fueled by passion, not money," John said repeatedly to the classes at Harvard, pushing his students to paths that would bring them long term satisfaction and fulfillment.

A heavy secretary with cat-eyeglasses and a shift dress escorted me to a small dusty office. Her large thighs made swishing sounds as I followed her down the long narrow hallway. Every few feet she would turn back checking to see that I was still behind her.

"Would you like some coffee, young man?" said the secretary with a grin displaying a wide space between her two front teeth.

"No thank you ma'am," I said.

"Mr. Brenner will be with you in just a minute or two. Kindly make yourself comfortable," she said as she chewed a sizeable glob of pink bubblegum.

She closed the door slowly eyeing me all the while as if she could see me, but I couldn't see her. She produced a rather large bubble which managed to get tangled up between the door frame and the now closed door. I pretended to look at something out the window while she opened the door to retrieve the pink string that decorated the door frame.

The desk in the small room was a haphazard mess, covered in papers and half empty Styrofoam cups of coffee. Boxes stacked on top one another filled the stale office nearly to the ceiling. A faded diploma from Charleston School of Law 1937 hung on the wall along with several pictures of Don Brenner posing with several local government officials. A camping family photo caught my eye and I picked it up to get a closer look. Mr. and Mrs. Brenner, side by side, with four children: three towheads and a tall one with a perfectly round Afro. A closeup of the photo revealed strong similarities between Mrs. Brenner and the dark one. Names on the boxes were handwritten in fat black marker: Leona Van Theil, Lester Calder, Pritchard Kelly and Brandon Thompson.

A commotion in the hallway and banging at the door brought me to my feet and I quickly grabbed the handle and swung open the door. A white-haired man with a handlebar moustache and crooked bowtie fell into me with a stack of files knocking me backward and onto the floor. I quickly got to my feet apologizing as I reached for the files and papers strewn everywhere.

"Well, well, Brenner said with a soft chuckle.

"You must be Rudy's boy!"

"Yes, sir," I said tucking in my shirt and straightening my jacket.

"Name's Donny, Donny Brenner," he said with an outstretched bear of a hand.

"Have a seat young man, while I sneak a cigarette."

"You see, Melanie, my secretary, won't let me smoke in the office, so I need to wait till she takes a lunch," he said.

"Don't mind, do you, son?" he asked.

He lit the cigarette before I could answer and flicked a switch that turned on a noisy overhead ventilator that produced an annoying scraping sound and little else.

"No," I said with a muffled cough as a cloud of smoke enveloped us.

Donny had a few puffs and then put out the cigarette in a glass ashtray he kept hidden in a small side drawer. He leaned back in his chair and looked at me with a hard stare for several moments before he spoke.

"So, tell me son, what is it that makes you interested in working in a thankless job with lousy pay?" he asked.

"If you've come looking for trial experience, this isn't the place," he barked.

"I'm fighting for the life of an innocent young man in one of those boxes right there and I don't have time to play games with the son of Rudolph Campbell," he said with eyes that squinted.

"See, I know Rudy Campbell and I know he could set you up real nice," he said.

"Now you tell me right now what you're doing here," said Donny while leaning forward with his arms crossed and elbows resting on the desk.

"I'm not. I'm not here for the trial experience."

"I... I don't care about the money," I stuttered.

Brenner didn't believe me. He raised his thunderous voice and stood to his feet.

"I got a poor kid sitting in jail for years on weak evidence. Kid's a throw away, got nobody... no visitors, no help at all... just me," he said pounding his chest while he paced.

"They picked him out and decided he was the one. Bigoted community and prosecutor and all of them puttin' pressure on a young D.A.," he said.

"Now they're all happy as pigs in dirt just to have a conviction. Don't give a damn that they got the wrong one!" he shouted, slamming his hand hard on the top of a box labeled Brandon Michael Thompson.

I jerked as his thunderous voice pierced through me. He was mad as Hell, and I pitied whoever got in his way. He finished his tyrant and sat back down and looked me in the eye, and it was right then and there I decided I wanted to work for Don Brenner.

IT WAS past midnight when I arrived back at the mansion. The glow of a cigarette in the dark drew my eyes to the stable. She sat on a wood bench staring up at the night sky cradling a cigarette burned nearly to the filter.

Hearing the crunch of my shoes on the gravel, she turned.

"Hi there," she said.

"What cha doing out here," I said with a sigh as I sat down letting all the air out of my lungs, exhausted.

"Couldn't sleep," she said as she pushed her cigarette down into the small ashtray stomping out each ember one by one.

"Where've you been all day"? she asked.

"I had some business in town is all."

Jean was sharp. She knew when someone was trying to weasel their way out of something. It was no use trying to lie.

"You don't want to work for him, do you? she asked.

"I can tell, and I don't blame you."

"How do you always know," I said.

"A mother knows," she said with a wink.

"Don't worry, I won't tell him. He only wants to hear what he wants to hear anyway," she said.

The tone of her voice was somehow different, and I sensed a change in her.

"How do you do it, mom," I said looking directly at her.

"How do you live here and do...," I said.

"Do what? Survive?" she snapped, turning away.

"No, no, I... I didn't mean it that way," I said, regretting my words.

"I'm sorry... that's... that's not how I meant it," I said moving to sit near her.

"I mean, you know how *he* is," I said softly.

She thought for a minute before she replied.

"I know what he is, Des. I know," she said nodding.

Our eyes met and her smile told me we were good.

She looked up at the sky and reached over to squeeze my hand while a bright flash of light burned its way through the galaxy.

It was just past 11:00am and they were both waiting for me as I entered the kitchen.

"Good morning, how about some coffee," said Jean while stealing glimpses of Rudy.

"Thanks."

Rudy put down his paper and checking his watch, got right to the point.

"So, Des, let's talk about your joining the firm," he said bluntly.

"I've already spoken to the partners, and everything is all set."

"We have a nice office and a secretary all set up for you," he said without looking at me.

"Uh, well... I, I wanted to talk to you about that too," I said.

"You'll begin working with a few of our smaller clients and then after a year or so, we'll transition over to the larger ones and bump up your salary," he said.

"But I need to uh, I'm not," I stammered.

Rudy continued, ignoring my pleas and I could feel the anger begin to rise inside of me.

"But wait, listen," I said.

Still, he pressed.

"We'll get you set up on a travel schedule so you can meet all of the clients face to face starting in New York and then we'll work our way down," he said.

I could feel my face flush as the anger intensified.

"You're not listening, dad," I said louder, slamming my mug on the table harder than I had intended.

Jean stopped what she was doing and stood near the doorway nervously rubbing her hands as she watched us.

"We should head over to the country club this afternoon and play golf with the other partners," he said.

"So, head upstairs and get dressed; we'll leave here in an hour," he barked.

"No! This is my life. I won't work there, not now. Not ever!" I shouted.

"You never asked me how I felt or what I wanted," I yelled.

"This is not about you!" I cried.

Rudy stood up and glared at me with a gaze I had never witnessed before.

"You will do exactly as I say," he said in a slow, threatening pace.

"No... I won't," I said shaking my head and never taking my eyes off his.

Rudy's face flushed red, and his fists clenched tight. Suddenly, he grabbed his coffee mug and flung it past me through the kitchen hitting the beveled glass window shattering it.

"Stop, it please, both of you!" Jean cried.

Rudy lunged towards me, and I pushed a barstool in front of me blocking his reach. Losing his balance, he tumbled over it and landed on the floor hitting his head. Jean fell to her knees and reached for him as he lay on the floor. A small trickle of blood sliding down his temple as his hands shook touching his head.

"Get away from me," he shouted pushing Jean away.

She sat on the floor with her hands covering her face crying while he grappled for the table lifting himself to his feet in a wobbly stance.

"I'm sorry. I just can't..." I began.

"Get out. Get out of my house!" he shouted.

"Get out of my house!" he screamed, eyes wild and bulging.

I flew up the stairs two at a time and grabbed everything I could tossing it in a duffle bag. He was still hollering when I threw open the front door and leapt past the gardens, fountain and around to the driveway. I reached the car and lunged at the handle, locking myself inside. My hands were still shaking as I drove through Charleston and Tennison Park for nearly three hours. I had finally calmed down and found a small diner with cheap food. The greasy burger was good enough, but the beer was perfect. I decided to talk to Brenner again and headed over to Legal Aid, but found the doors locked and the parking lot empty. I drove around some more and finally, with the needle on empty, I pulled over across the street from the Tennison Park Bus Terminal. With no money and no clue what to do next, I killed the ignition and took a deep breath, resting my head on the steering wheel. I don't know how long I dozed, but I woke to someone tapping on the passenger side window. The police officer looked at me with suspicion and I leaned over and rolled down the window.

"You can't sleep here," he hollered.

"Move along," he barked while eyeing me closely before heading down the sidewalk to check the other vehicles parked illegally along Tremont Street.

The Tennison Park bus terminal was bustling with activity. Grey Hounds arrived and parked for the night while others idled at the curb waiting on passengers for redeyes heading east. Arriving passengers exited one by one with handbags and luggage into the arms of family members or no one at all. Some were greeted with hugs and colorful bouquets while others exited by themselves leaving the terminal alone. It was getting dark, and I figured it was best to find a well-lit parking lot someplace other than Tennison Park.

I turned the ignition and just as I began to pull away, I saw her standing there. I cranked the window down to get a better look. She was under the streetlamp clutching a small white suitcase as the last Greyhound hissed and started its descent. She was pregnant and appeared lost. Her long hair flowed to her waist as her stomach accentuated the bottom half of a printed maternity smock. I couldn't believe my eyes, Leah, was right here in Charleston! I left the curb like a maniac and pulled up alongside her. She smiled when she saw me, and I melted instantly. It had been months, and I was more than thrilled to see Leah. I moved my things into the back and helped her inside. She started to cry, and I pulled her tight.

"I can't believe you're here," I said.

"How did you know?" she said.

"I didn't!" I said hugging her.

She was tired from the two-day bus ride, and I had to figure out how to get her some food and a proper place to sleep for the night. Campbell Mansion was out of the question.

IT WAS dark when I knocked on the front door of the small Cape Cod. The door opened and a massive Golden Retriever jumped out and onto me, his tail wagging a mile a minute as he greeted me with licks to the face.

"I guess he likes you," said a woman in a tie dye t-shirt, faded jeans and grayish-black hair to her waist.

"I guess he does," I said supporting the Golden who was now at eye level.

Donny Brenner came to the door in his robe and slippers looking surprised and annoyed.

"What are you doing here?" he said.

"Well, I uh... I... wanted to tell you that I... I accept the position," I said even though we both knew he hadn't yet made the offer.

"What the...," he began and then stopped when he noticed Leah's belly.

Brenner perused the two of us as well as my car which was filled with pretty much everything I owned before he relented and opened the door.

A warm breeze drifted over the porch of the Brenner home while Donny and I drank beer. I told him Leah and I met at Harvard and the events that led to our breakup and now, subsequent back togetherness.

"I was a jerk" I said.

"I did well at Harvard and got a lot of recognition. Then....it went to my head, and I lost her. I had no idea she was pregnant!"

"Sometimes it starts out rocky," Brenner said with a knowing smile.

"But you have to keep at it—don't let it go, it's worth the work," he said confidently.

"The missus and I started out that way too... it was a big mess," he said with a wave of his hand.

"When we met, she already had a baby from a young Negro boy from high school. Her first love," he said.

"As soon as the boy found out she was pregnant, he bolted as fast as he could. Her parents did the same thing," he said.

"We met at the laundromat just up the street when Eva was just one year old," he said with a smile.

"After that, it was just the three of us against the world. But we made it work and I love her daughter as if she were my own blood."

"Wouldn't trade it for anything now, but back then... whew... it was tough," he said.

Inhaling from a fat cigar he pushed a perfectly round smoke ring into the air as white moths fluttered in and out of the fading circle. We started a second beer and talked late into the night and the more I got to know Don Brenner, the more I liked him.

After breakfast he handed me some bills as an advance on my salary and told me where I could find a low rent apartment. Leah and I found a small one-bedroom place two blocks from the Legal Aid Bureau and sifted through secondhand stores for furniture, kitchen supplies and anything else affordable. Donny gave us the mattress and box springs from his guest room, and we made the small apartment our own as best we could.

It was Friday night, and I was exhausted. I came home to find Leah had set up a candlelight dinner on a small cardboard box in the center of the living room. I finished a beer and set the empty bottle horizontal on the makeshift table spinning it in a playful game of truth or dare. The nose of the bottle landed directly on Leah, and I called "truth." Leah smiled at me the way she always did saying I love you with just her eyes. I needed to ask her but at the same time, fearing what she might say. I knew I had to tread carefully so I came around to her side of the box and put one arm around her and another on top of her large belly. She leaned into me and rested her head on my shoulder closing her eyes. It was getting closer to her due date and with each passing day, she was increasingly tired.

"Why did you wait so long," I said softly in her ear.

She opened her eyes and thought for a moment before she answered.

"I... I wasn't sure if you would want this," she said casting her eyes away from me.

I brushed my knuckles along her cheek.

"What? Why would you think that?" I asked.

"Because you had changed, Des...." she said as her eyes filled.

"But you wouldn't return my calls. If you had told me, I would have," I said.

"What Des, you would have what?" she asked.

"You know I have to ask. I have to know, Leah. It won't change how I feel about you or the baby, but I have to know," I said.

She sat up and faced me. She didn't speak for a minute, searching my eyes, one and then the other. Finally, she spoke.

"Yes, Des, it's yours... the baby is yours," she said.

She then nestled into me resting her head on my shoulder. I kissed her head and we held one another until the candle's flame was enveloped by wax and a thin string of gray smoke rose to the ceiling.

Sixteen

Legal Aid had a backlog of cases, but Brenner wanted me to focus on one case in particular that was keeping him up at night. A young boy convicted of the murder of a young girl was on his fourth of a forty-year sentence. According to Brenner, a weak alibi and incompetent legal team had botched the case. Evidence against Brandon Thompson was frail at best and Brenner felt the former defense team had failed miserably.

It was past 7:00pm and the thunderstorm was wreaking havoc on the electricity causing sporadic outages in the tired old building. I finished the last of two Buttermilk doughnuts and started on the Thompson case by arranging files into chronological stacks. The piles of documents were big enough to fill a small closet. With all the information I wondered what had swayed the jury to convict Brandon Thompson in just twenty-four hours.

The wind rattled old windows creating a steady whistle through broken calk as the storm became more violent. For the third time, the electricity was interrupted leaving the room completely black, and I reached aimlessly in the dark for the table's edge. She was right behind me when the lights came back on, and I quickly turned and ran straight into her.

"Ah!" I screamed as I flew into the table, ending up on the other side of it and against the wall like a hissing cat ready to strike.

Somehow, Melanie had entered the small office without a sound.

"I done scared ya, did I"? she said giggling freely. She covered a wide grin with one hand in an attempt to control herself. Apparently, my gymnastics routine was hilarious.

"Yeah, you did," I said with a pathetic chuckle and pending heart attack.

"Well, Mr., don't you work too much longer," she scolded wagging a thick index finger under my nose.

"That pretty little girl of yours is about to pop!"

"I won't, I promise. Thanks for the doughnuts... um... they were really great," I said.

Melanie came in close and gave me a bear hug and peck on the cheek. She wished me a good night and then, in an apparent flashback, began to giggle again.

She blew me a kiss and waved goodbye as she exited the office turning off lights while making her way to the small parking lot and rusty VW Beetle. I picked up the last folder labeled C.P.D. Confidential, the contents of which had sailed onto the floor and underneath a wide desk. On my knees, I reached for a photograph and scooped it up along with clumps of dust and paperclips. As I brushed the dust off my clothes, the storm once again turned the small office to complete darkness.

"Not again," I said reaching for the edge of the desk.

A loud crack of thunder and burst of lightening illuminated the worn photograph for a split second and fear began to race through my veins. Another burst of lightening filled the office, and I began to panic. The face, pale white had blood red eyes that stared back at me. I threw the photograph of Tessa Rhodes and backed away from it knocking over a vase that crashed to the floor sending water and shards of glass everywhere. My body began to tremble, and my hands shook uncontrollably. Again, the thunder pounded the sky and lightening illuminated the dark office. I dropped to my knees reaching for the other photographs as the lights came back on. My heart pounded out of my chest and sweat drenched my forehead and neck. There were deep red and purple ligature marks on her neck wide and defined as a testament to his rage. Her lips were swollen and bruised, and the whites of her eyes were completely red and eerily lifeless. As thunder pounded the night sky, I pulled the waste can under me just in time losing everything I had ingested with the realization I would be defending Brandon Thompson, the monster convicted of killing Tessa Rhodes.

When I arrived home, Leah was at the kitchen sink. I came up behind her and hugged her tighter than ever while burying my face in her neck..

"I'll always protect you. I'll never leave you... ever," I whispered.

She turned to see my swollen eyes and dropping her towel, she lifted my face and held it in her hands. She kissed my forehead and cradled my head as I sobbed.

BRENNER ENTERED my office and closed the door behind him. He sat down and lifted his feet onto a small ottoman lighting a cigarette that sent smoke sailing up to the ceiling and into the blades of a dusty fan.

"So... what are your thoughts on the Thompson case?" he asked.

His keen eyes were on me searching beyond my words and I could see he was contemplating whether he should keep me on the case.

"Evidence is weak. Not enough for a conviction," I said.

"Looks like Brandon Thompson was the best they had, and they went for it," I said.

"I want to talk to him. I need to know more about him and trace his steps the day Tessa was killed," I said.

"He's holding something back. There's got to be more. I need to see him face to face," I said.

Brenner turned and studied me with a hard gaze.

"You knew her, Des?" he asked.

"Yes," I stammered.

"I knew her," I said softly.

It was naive of me to think he wouldn't find out.

"She, she was a friend, and I...well, I liked her," I said.

"If you let your own feelings get in the way, you're done," he said sharply.

"I understand," I said.

"I think we can win, but I need to see him. I need to look in his eyes," I said.

Again, he studied me and after a long pause, finally relented.

"Ok, you go see him, but damn it, don't you dare come back here and take this on if you're not gonna fight tooth and nail," he threatened.

"I want this boy out of prison," he warned as he got up and left the room.

I spent the next two months combing through piles of documents on the Thompson case. Brenner wanted a detailed assessment before we would file an appeal to have the case reconsidered. Brandon had spent a good deal of time at the railroad tracks near Tennison Park close to where Tessa was found. He lived on and off with an aunt and spent time at the tracks and slept in the boxcars on occasion. Brandon had a criminal record of theft at several of the local stores and markets but no history of violence or sexual misconduct. Those that knew him described Brandon as invisible...a loner with no real family or friends. According to the records, Brandon lied repeatedly about his whereabouts the day Tessa was killed. He said he was nowhere near the tracks, but he was seen running from the tracks shortly after the coroner's estimated time of death. Brandon said he never saw Tessa, but it was proved he did see her at the Tennison Park basketball courts on several occasions, even talking with her. Weak defense coupled with his lying earned him forty years in Lee Correctional Institute.

Over the next few weeks Brenner and I would prepare a motion, but first I would talk to everyone that was involved in the case. The records indicated Combs had interrogated Brandon on several occasions, but nothing in his notes indicated he thought Brandon was the killer. Charleston Police Department was a small, outdated office with ten desks in an open area and a long reception counter that separated civilians from the officers and detectives. A Negro police officer named Charlene was at reception when I arrived. She was a heavy woman with thick arms and a hard demeanor. She looked me over stoically and turned towards a detective sitting at a corner desk in the back.

"He's here," she said matter of fact, glancing at me again with an icy stare while the rest of the pack ogled me like a criminal. Mumbling to one another, they assessed me while I stood there in awkward silence. I studied the floor tiles while Combs took his time with the phone call. Finally, he hung up the phone and stood to his feet, puffing his chest like a rooster in a hen house.

"Desmond Campbell?" he said loudly.

"Thee Desmond Campbell?" he mused.

The entire office roared in laughter along with Combs. I could feel my face flush red and my body tense.

"Well, well, come on in, Mr. Campbell. To what do we owe this honor?" he said with a mocking head bow.

Combs continued with the comedy show to the amusement of the other officers and detectives. I walked through the jeers and smirks to the back of the office and stood in front of him. When the room finally quieted, I began.

"Well... Detective Combs. It appears you arrested the wrong guy," I said loud enough for the rest of the office to hear. Ray's smile quickly vanished, and his demeanor turned serious. The other detectives quieted and some quickly found things to do in other areas of the office. Apparently, I had struck a nerve with Ray, and I was more than pleased to prove to him that he couldn't push me around and get away with it. Ray sat down and motioned for me to sit in a chair across from him.

"What the hell are you talking about," said Ray.

"Brandon Thompson," I said.

"Jury found him guilty."

"We don't think he is," I said.

I watched as the muscles in Ray's jaw flexed and his nostrils flared.

"We think the evidence is weak and we're going for an appeal. I came to ask for your help," I said, hoping my humble approach would allow his ego to rest, but he wasn't done.

"So, the rich white kid with a big shot daddy has come to save the day. Is that right, Mr. Campbell?" he said.

"We don't think he did it. We think he was wrongly convicted, detective, and we want him out," I said politely holding back the anger I felt at his insults.

He stood abruptly.

"Get the hell out of my office, and don't come back here," he roared.

"Punk lawyer! Get your white royal ass out of my office now!" he shouted.

Ray Combs shook me to the core, and I was rattled pretty bad. In a haste to get out of there, my briefcase strap got tangled up on a metal chair and it tumbled over with a loud clang. All eyes upon me, I raced to the front door nearly tripping as I yanked at the handle.

"Dare question my authority"!" he shouted into a silent room.

I KISSED Leah as she slept and quietly stuffed a notepad and a small recorder into a briefcase as I headed out the door at 7:00am on Saturday. The drive to Lee Correctional Institute in Bishopville would take about two hours each way and I wanted enough time with Brandon to assess his character and dig further into what he remembered about the day Tessa was killed. I made a promise to myself. If at any time I felt the slightest hint that he may be guilty, I would stop and remove myself from the case.

Four Corrections officers were huddled around a smut magazine when I entered the facility. I stood at the counter for minutes before they were finally able to tear themselves away. Three of them headed over to their stations without acknowledging me. The fourth one glared stone faced as I slid my I.D. under the glass window.

"546912 Thompson," said the officer to the others. They pulled a file on Brandon Thompson that held his photo and credentials and confirmed I was on the visitation list. With a loud buzz, the heavy steel doors opened and closed with a loud clang.

"Stand in there," the C.O. shouted, pointing to a small sterile room with concrete flooring and clear glass walls. An aggressive canine was brought into the room, and it immediately dug its nose into my legs and torso searching for any trace of contraband.

"Whoa," I said as the Shepherd's paws hit my chest, its nose perusing the length of my torso. The guards continued their suspicious assessment while they patted me down. They grabbed my briefcase from my hands to inspect the contents.

"Get 546912 over to visitor. His lawyer is here," said one guard as he hung up the phone.

I was taken to another small room to wait while they located Brandon. It was almost an hour before one of the guards finally opened the door from the visiting area and called my name.

"Follow me," commanded the guard.

We entered a large room with concrete floors filled with rows of stationery table and chair units. I sat down at a small stool at the only open table and waited. Thick cigarette smoke throughout the room made my eyes water and caused me to sneeze repeatedly. Well-armed Corrections Officers stationed in each corner of the room continually monitored the activity of the almost completely Negro population. My anxiety was growing as I waited and all I could think about were the photos of Tessa and how brutally she was killed. I recounted with clarity her blood red eyes and the purple strangulation marks on her neck. I looked around at the prisoners and felt anger welling up inside me. The inmates appeared to enjoy themselves, holding hands with visitors and chatting with relatives. All the while an invisible victim somewhere on the outside suffered or lay dead. These men were confined, but at least they had their lives. Tessa never had the chance to graduate, marry or have a family of her own, and I began to doubt what I was doing here. What if he did kill her...what if Brandon was faking his innocence and all of this was for nothing? What if I was just another idiot waiting to talk with a murderer who would later be released only to kill again?

I sat waiting for nearly a half hour when across the room a door opened, and a guard brought in a young man in bright orange attire that I assumed was Brandon Thompson. Compared to the other prisoners, he was small framed and appeared shy and scared. His eyes scanned the room as if it were his first time in the visitor center or perhaps, he was assessing the room for any sign of danger. I stood up as they walked towards the table and before the guard left, he barked at us.

"Half hour, that's it," said the C.O.

Brandon and I stood looking at one another for several seconds before I introduced myself, reaching to shake his hand. He nodded but didn't oblige the handshake and in awkward silence we sat down. I was nervous.

"I'm part of the Legal Aid team and I, uh... well, we want to get you out of here," I said hopeful and with the assumption he would be pleased.

There was no reaction from Brandon. He was quiet and seemed to have trouble making eye contact. A wide bruise around his right eye and several abrasions on his chin and arms told me he had enemies here. He seemed to wince at the bright light in the room and I wondered if he spent most of his time in his cell or solitary confinement.

"You got cigarettes?" he said suddenly.

"Uh, no," I said. "I... I don't smoke," I said realizing he was more interested in a smoke than my helping him.

He looked disappointed and continued to scan the room for something or someone. I was starting to get frustrated and decided it was best to get right to the point. We didn't have much time and I needed him to focus.

"Look, if we're gonna do this, I need you to help me. I did three months of research and drove two hours to see you and I need you to think about that day and tell me everything......every single detail of where you were and what you did and who you saw," I said.

"Junk lawyer," he said looking at me with disgust.

He then continued scanning the room, ignoring me. I was rattled by the insult but decided to try another approach. I would meet him at his level. If I could get him to see me as an ally, maybe I could get him to talk.

"I know you didn't do it, but I can't get you out until we figure out who did. I can't do this without you... we have to work as a team or we can't do it at all," I pleaded.

He stopped scanning the room and looked at me hard.

"She wasn't killed by me," he said angrily.

"Rich bigots got the trashy white kid, now they're happy, and you're one too," he said defiantly.

"No... no, I'm not," I stammered.

"I am *not* one of them," I said shaking my head.

Now I was mad, and he could see it. He seemed to like it that I wasn't afraid of him, and I began to get a sense that he would talk so I pushed onward.

"You were running from the tracks a short time after she was killed," I said clearing my throat.

"There were a lot of witnesses that identified you. What were you running from?" I asked.

He looked at me and I could see he was thinking about it and then slowly he began to talk. Brandon leaned forward on the table with one hand holding the side of his head while he spoke.

"I was afraid... I slept in the boxcar that night and I was afraid they would find me in there and get me on trespassing or some other bull. I headed through the woods towards T-Park. Nobody was ever in the woods," he said shaking his head.

"I hear something behind me...in between the booms; it sounded like... a female... muffled sound like a scream and then it was quiet, and I got scared. I was looking behind me but still going forward fast and that's when I run straight into him," he said.

"A large white guy with dark hair and a big sweaty face; angry looking" he said.

"I thought he was F.R.A. authority and was gonna mess me up, so I ran the other way as fast as I could," he said.

"I saw Main Street and kept going. I ran through the street parade, the July 4th Street Fest, and across the street. All the people were looking at me like, what's this kid doing... what's he running for?" he said.

I hadn't noticed that I stopped writing as I listened intently to Brandon. There were over twenty witnesses that day that identified Brandon Thompson as the one running from the woods. Brandon was sharp and he remembered a lot. I began to jot down a detailed description of the big guy, location and timing. When I asked him about ever seeing Tessa, he confessed, he saw her at the basketball court and even spoke to her. He didn't lie to me, and I was relieved. I began to trust him. He told me why he slept in the boxcars and hung his head when he recounted the time he spent at his aunt's home in the old Victorian. By the time we finished, I believed what he said and vowed to give it my all to get him out of L.C.I.

I returned to Charleston late that night stopping halfway in Holly Hill at a small diner and used the pay phone to call Leah. I didn't want to be away from her too long as the baby was due any day now. I would call Jean and Rudy after the baby was born as a courtesy, but I didn't want them a part of our lives. It would be hard with the baby and all on our own, but in the long run, their influence would only aggravate an already volatile situation.

Seventeen

It was just before midnight on New Year's Eve when I heard her scream. Leah was bent over with a pinkish puddle underneath her as she cradled her stomach and leaned into the sink. I jumped out of bed and helped her over to a chair and dressed as fast as I could. We got into the car and sped to Charleston Memorial Hospital racing through signal lights and stop signs frantic to get to the hospital before the baby came. I could tell she was close as the pain was more frequent and more intense with each contraction. We were both scared.

Leah screamed at the same time the tires screeched to a halt in front of the E.R. I raced into the hospital and ran back to the car with two nurses in tow. We helped Leah into a wheelchair, and she was whisked into labor and delivery instantly. I waited while they prepped her and paced in the small waiting area for hours before the nurse finally motioned for me to come in. I stopped just inside the doorway. A ray of sunlight from the small window stretched across the quiet room illuminating the bed. He was wrapped in a faint blue blanket and was asleep in her arms. They were the most beautiful thing I had ever seen, and I could barely move.

We were a big hit with the local press having the first baby born in the New Year. They stayed in our room for most of the afternoon filming and taking photographs of the first grandchild of Rudolph Campbell born on New Year's Day.

"Get in closer together now you two," said a news reporter.

"That's it, perfect!" he said as the photographer snapped one blinding flash after another.

"Are you going to name him Rudolph Campbell the Second," said the little guy with the Grand Canyon smile and microphone at my mouth.

"Uh…." is all I could say as the camera man moved in closer zeroing in on my blank expression while my exhausted eyes darted back and forth from one crew member to another.

"Cut!" said the reporter.

"Ok then. Let's try that one more time," he said with a feeble grin.

LEAH AND the baby were both sound asleep when I left Charleston Memorial just before dusk. I barely made it to my car when he spoke.

"You look good on TV," he said from behind me.

I turned to see Ray Combs leaning against the side of a car, his arms folded neatly across his chest.

"I have a new baby boy!"

He smiled and walked over to shake my hand.

"Congratulations," said Ray Combs.

"Thanks. It was a close one. I thought we were going to have him in the front seat," I said.

"What's his name?" asked Ray.

"We don't know yet. We couldn't decide, and then all of a sudden he was here!"

Ray smiled and walked back toward his car and then stopped and turned around.

"You working for Don Brenner?" he asked.

"Yes sir, I am," I said.

"He's a good man," said Ray as he chewed on a toothpick.

"I have some information that might interest you," said Ray before he turned to walk away.

"Ok, ok!" I said.

I was eager for whatever it was he had to say but didn't want to push him.

He gave me the thumbs up as he walked with his back to me towards an old Chevy Impala with a cracked windshield.

I proposed to Leah on a blanket in Battery Park on a warm Saturday in September. We watched children playing ball, people reading books and joggers sprinting past sunbathers and curious tourists. An elderly couple inched their way along the boardwalk hand in hand, stopping every so often to watch the sailboats glide across the Ashley River. An oversized silk scarf tied at her chin, the tails of which were periodically grabbed by the river breeze to rest on her companion's nose. Each time it did that they would stop, and he would remove the scarf from his face and turn to smile at her. That's what it's all about, I thought.... watching boats and taking walks and spending the rest of your life with someone that you love. After all we had been through, I couldn't believe she still loved me.

Leah played peek-a-boo with Christopher as he squirmed in the center of a soft blanket. Her hands covered her eyes before every burst of "boo," and he giggled every time as if it were the very first time. He never got tired of that game or maybe it was his mother that he never tired of. He couldn't get enough of her and neither could I. When she uncovered her eyes and shouted a final "boo," I was ready. A bright diamond sat propped in a box on Christopher's tummy. I shifted upward to rest on one knee and reached for her hand. She stopped suddenly and turned her eyes to mine, her free hand lifting to her cheek. We drew a small crowd and earned an applause from the bystanders when she said yes and hugged my neck pulling me tumbling onto the blanket.

We were married in Charleston City Hall three weeks later. The bells of St. Andrews Church echoed through the city and a white veil flew behind us as we made our way down the steps of the historic building.

Eighteen

I met a tired looking Ray Combs at a pub that bordered Charleston and Tennison Park. Inhabited mainly by locals, it was old, dingy and the perfect spot for our meeting. The pub was nestled inside a poorer neighborhood with cobblestone streets and brownstones shoulder to shoulder along narrow avenues. There were broken or burned-out streetlamps and rundown apartment buildings decorated with rows of colorful laundry that danced on string three stories high. I spotted him at the bar and sat down one stool over listening while he and the bartender bickered over the draft picks and who was going to do what to whom. Ray, with empty glasses in front of him, was already on his third scotch. He must have downed them so quickly the bartender hadn't the time to clean up in between customers. Detective Combs looked exhausted and miserable. He rubbed his eyes fervently for several seconds while I ordered a beer. We moved to a table towards the back of the bar and Ray began to tell me what he knew about Brandon Thompson.

"How's your boy?" he asked with a twinkle in his eye.

"Great... he's just great," I said.

"Leah, well she's tired, you know, but we're having a ball, we just love him so much."

"I can't wait to get home at night to see him, but work is long and most of the time he's already asleep," I said.

Ray Combs was somehow different now. I didn't like him at first, not at all. He was rude and arrogant. But now, I sensed I was seeing the real Ray Combs and I liked this version of him better.

"I never knew my father," he said staring at the scotch in his glass.

"It's a big deal to have a son and to be grateful for that child," he said now looking at me, but sort of through me at the same time.

"All children are important... they all matter," he said with conviction and a scar of tangible pain.

"Brandon Thompson matters too," he said with a long sigh.

It was obvious this had been a tough case for him.

"The Thompson boy was all they had. I had some other leads, some other stones unturned, but they wouldn't let me get in there," he said shaking his head.

"I was on to something and needed more time, but the D.A. and Chief, well they wanted this thing wrapped up quick," he said snapping his fingers.

"There was pressure coming from somewhere else, but I don't know where or why," he said with a cold stare.

"All of a sudden, they were pushing hard to get it solved, and they didn't seem to want to know anything," he said followed by a generous swallow of scotch.

Combs, with creased brow, continued.

"The kid was in the wrong place at the wrong time, and he had no one to vouch for him. The young boy came from nothing and had no one to help him except a couple of low-rate attorneys that barely made it out of law school," said Ray.

"I was pulled from the case without reason and before I knew it, they had a conviction," he said.

"Brandon Thompson won't let me sleep at night, and I need to sleep," he said with sallow eyes and an unshaven face.

It seemed the tables had somehow turned, and Ray Combs was now asking for *my* help. We walked out the back where his car was parked in a dark corner of the small lot. He shook my hand and then grabbed a file from the trunk pushing it inside my jacket.

"Look into this for me, won't you kid?" he said.

He patted my arm just below my shoulder twice and then got in his car and turned the engine on. I stood in the dark clinging tight to the confidential folder at my chest as I watched him pull away.

I DUG into the documents from Ray, reviewing them meticulously over and over. Ray's conversations with Mr. Rhodes revealed an anonymous admirer that had sent roses to Tessa regularly. Who was this admirer and why did they send the flowers with an unsigned card?

I arrived home to find an empty apartment and a be-home-soon note from Leah next to a big bouquet of yellow roses. The note from Page's Floristry said "Congratulations! Can't wait to meet him! Rudy and Jean." I had a sick feeling in my stomach. Our celebrity in the local paper no doubt alerted them to Christopher's arrival sooner than I would have liked.

Begrudgingly, I would bring Leah and the baby to the mansion to meet Rudy and Jean. That day had now come. My stomach in knots, I pulled on my suit jacket while Leah tied her hair in a tight bun at the base of her neck. I watched her from the bed as she dabbed a hint of rouge high on her cheekbones and then onto her lips. Sun bleached strands of hair surrounded her face and curled lazily on her shoulders. She inserted a small pearl earring in one earlobe and then the other. Her skin, bronze and flawless was remarkable. Leah didn't fuss much with her appearance. She didn't have to. She was a natural beauty.

"You're quiet," she said turning around to examine me.

"I hate this," I said while struggling with my tie.

"Which do you hate more, the tie or the visit," she said coming over to lend a hand.

Leah pushed the knot upward, centering it between my shirt-collar. She pressed the material with her hand from top to bottom smoothing the ripples then looked deep into my eyes, searching.

"We have to go," she said.

"He's their grandson and it's a good excuse to see them and bury the hatchet."

"We'll be out of there before you know it. Give me a sign when you've had enough, and I'll get us out of there," she said with a wink.

I pulled her to me and kissed her lips and then pulled her into a tight hug, kissing her head.

"This is your parents' house!" Leah exclaimed as I parked the car under the shade of a towering Oak.

I pulled her to me playfully kissing her neck and whispered in her ear.

"If we do away with them, it's all ours," I joked.

"All three of you and it's all mine!" she trumped, pushing me away with a giggle.

I reached over to touch her face with my palm. I was so grateful to have her. Christopher let out a loud happy shriek and we turned around to tickle his tiny feet.

Soon we stood at the front entry nervously waiting. Massive white pillars stood behind us on the wide porch like giant Roman guards protecting the fortress. Jean opened the door with a display of enthusiasm, the likes of which I had never seen. In her excitement, she dropped her dish towel on the ground and instinctively reached for Christopher.

"He's just perfect," she gushed holding him and bouncing him lightly as we walked through the grand foyer towards the formal dining room.

"Mother, this is Leah," I said.

"Oh, I'm so embarrassed! It's so nice to meet you," Jean said reaching for Leah's hand.

"No worries at all," said Leah as she perused the mansion.

"He has that effect on people!"

Christopher was a happy baby and didn't mind being held by strangers. They feel like strangers to me too, I thought as we walked through the wide hallway into the kitchen. Leah helped ease some of the awkwardness at having to see my parents for the first time after the fight. I could hear Rudy's heavy steps as he marched down the hallway and felt my gut begin to burn.

"Des how are you, son," as he reached to shake my hand.

He turned to Leah, kissed her on her cheek and then moved in close for a hug. Her chin touched his shoulder as his hands rested and then caressed slightly the curve of her waist before he released her. Her subtle discomfort and flushed cheeks were evident only to me.

'Get your filthy hands off her,' flashed through my mind as my fists clenched.

Rudy smiled at the baby touching his cheek and letting Christopher's tight grip envelop his fingers.

We sat down for dinner and Jean reminisced about me and how Christopher resembled me at the same age.

"Des was such a happy baby. I could take him anywhere and he always behaved so well," she bragged. "His hair was white-blonde, just like Christopher's!" she exclaimed.

Leah and Jean seemed to be at ease as though they had known one another for a long time. Dinner went better than expected, and Christopher was a delightful entertainer, keeping the underlying tension at bay. Rudy, never completely giving his full attention at any family gathering, periodically checked his watch.

'Need to be somewhere?' I thought, annoyed with his blatant self-importance.

We finished dessert while Jean fed Christopher small spoonsful of vanilla ice cream for the first time. Eyes wide, his sudden interest in the frosty treat kept the atmosphere jovial. Rudy was quiet but friendly and cordial throughout dinner. A break in the "baby talk" gave him an opportunity to ask me about my work at Legal Aid.

"It's good. Long hours and I'm exhausted most of the time, but I like it," I said carefully, not wanting to throw salt in the still vulnerable wound. I tried to direct the conversation away from my work, but for the third time Rudy circled back to it. He pushed to hear more about the Thompson case, his eyes darting away from mine with each inquiry.

"We think they convicted in error. There were other suspects, but the chief and D.A. were in a hurry to wrap things up," I said.

"Oh?" said Rudy with bridled curiosity. He held back for only a moment before he pushed further, asking for information he knew was confidential.

"Who are the other suspects?" he inquired.

I shifted uneasy in my chair hesitating and Leah took note.

"We have to get him to bed, Des." Leah said rescuing me with masterful sternness.

"Yep, ok," I said getting up. I helped Jean gather dishes and escorted her into the kitchen. When she had me alone, she jumped at the opportunity to tell me she was grateful to see the baby, and would we visit more? I promised to try and thanked her for the beautiful roses, giving her a light kiss on the cheek.

"Your father ordered those," she said as she straightened my collar and tie.

"You know, he never ever sent me roses!" she said.

"But I'm glad you and Leah liked them," she said with a pained smile.

"I'm so happy to see you both and the baby, he's just wonderful" said Jean hugging me.

"I want you to have this," she said pushing an envelope into my pocket.

"Don't... now don't tell your father, just take it," she said sternly.

"Promise me," she urged.

"Yes, yes, I promise."

I assumed the envelope was money, but I would wait till we got home to open it. Jean knew we were broke, and it was kind of her to help us. I didn't like taking anything from them and especially Rudy. I didn't want to owe them anything. It was enough that they had paid for school, and I was grateful not to have to try and come up with a few thousand dollars each month for student loan payments.

Rudy insisted on walking us out to the car. This, I surmised, was so he could drill me again about the Thompson case. We were quiet as we walked, and I thought that I might just get away without having to skirt around it again, but I was wrong. Sure enough, he made one last ditch effort.

"I'd like to help you with the case, Des," he said boldly.

"Why don't you come by the office this week and we'll talk about it. Happy to help out," he said smugly.

How was I going to get out of this one? Just as I was about to come up with a fabulous excuse, I decided to play his game.

"Ok, sure," I said.

"He's very interested in your work," Leah quipped as we got into the car, pulling the tie from her hair to let it flow freely onto her shoulders and waist.

"A little too interested," I said dryly.

Why was Rudy so interested in the Brandon Thompson case? Why was he pushing me so hard for information? I was puzzled. What did he ever care about a poor kid from Tennison Park? All tension left me as we pulled away from the mansion and drove through the beautiful tree lined streets of Charleston.

Christopher's sleeping face reflected in the rearview mirror made my heart swell and in that very moment, nothing else mattered. Once inside the apartment, Leah readied Christopher for bed and I poured a Guinness and stared at the blonde bubbles that floated up to rest in the white foam. The conversations with Rudy and Jean looped on auto play in my head. I was already having anxiety about meeting with Rudy and had to come up with a strategy...and fast. A faint scent of fruit and cloves drew my attention to the roses, and I grabbed the card from the table to reread the note from Page's Floristry. Interestingly, Page's Floristry was noted in Ray Combs' files on Brandon Thompson. I would visit the florist and see if I could find out more.

Nineteen

"Good afternoon," I said to the woman at the counter inside the floral shop. She was tapping quickly on a clunky adding machine with the end of a pencil while the other hand turned page after page with a lick of her thumb.

"Hello, just one second." she said with a smile.

She finished writing in a ledger and closed the book, securing it with the elastic string bound to the spine.

"What can I help you with?" said Donna Page.

"I'm Des Campbell with Legal Aid Bureau of Charleston," I said handing her my card.

"Do you mind if I ask you a few questions?"

"Sure, as long as you buy me a coffee," said Donna with a wink.

"I've been trying to take a break for the last three hours! I'm in desperate need of a coffee so I can keep going for a big shot wedding tomorrow!"

Donna and I walked to a small coffee shop, and she ordered a coffee with milk.

"Black with two sugars, please," I said to the red-haired girl at the counter.

We sat down across from each other on old Victorian chairs with faded velvet cushions.

"I've had the flower shop for over 25 years now. I don't have to work really. I don't need the money, but I love the flowers and making something special for my customers," she said.

"For many of them, it's their once in a lifetime event, and I have a part in that," she said proudly.

"I care about them, you know. I see the couples and hope they make it. Especially, the young ones, like you. They don't know what they're getting into really, and I wish I could tell them all these things that I've learned from my own mistakes. But you know, they have to go through it themselves," she said shaking her head with a smile.

"Well, I've talked way too much. What can I help you with, Des?"

"I'm trying to gather more evidence to overturn a conviction," I said.

"There were roses that were bought regularly for a young woman several years ago. We need to know who purchased them. Detective Ray Combs spoke with you and noted they were always paid for in cash," I said.

"That's right, yes, they were always paid for in cash. I thought it was odd, but I was always so busy, I didn't have much time to really think about it," she said.

"But, I remember," said Donna suddenly before she became quiet.

"I do recall one time his car wouldn't start, and he needed to get the flowers delivered that day! We called a tow service, and they came and got the car going again and then he left. I think it may have been Sawyer's Towing or," No, it was Buddy's... that's it, Buddy's!" she said.

Donna's recollection of the man matched verbatim the notes from Ray Combs. He was a big man with dark colored hair and a ruddy complexion. I thanked her and started to leave.

"Oh, one more thing," I said.

"Do you recall when he came in last... the very last time he came into the shop?"

Donna thought for a moment while she clicked the button on a retractable pen several times.

"I think it was near a holiday... hmmm... the Fourth of July, maybe," she said, clicking again.

"The county boys were hanging flags on the streetlamps all the way down Main Street that morning. I do remember that," she said.

"Everyone was excited for the parade... it's a big deal around here."

"Yes, now I remember!" she exclaimed.

"He came in on the Fourth of July and bought a dozen of my finest red roses. The shop was closed. and the curtains pulled tight. I was preparing some bouquets and was enjoying the solitude, but he kept knocking and knocking till finally I answered."

"He seemed desperate. That's the very last time I saw him," she said nodding.

BUDDY'S WRECKING was located on a dead-end street in an old industrial complex a few miles into North Charleston. The smell of oil and exhaust filled my nostrils immediately upon entering the shop. The pungent aroma and ensuing nausea caused me to cough spontaneously. The office and waiting area contained a beat-up vending machine, stained plastic chairs and a couple of old end tables. Ashtrays filled with cigarette butts and wrinkled copies of *Popular Mechanics* were piled up on small wobbly tables. Traces of oily fingerprints were dotted on every inch of the small shop that hadn't been swept in decades. Faded certificates and collision and repair pricing signs hung on dusty walls. A Raquel Welch poster with business cards fastened with push pins along the sides and bottom was taped to the door. Hendrix' "Purple Haze" could be heard from the dirty garage in between the sound of revving engines and clanging tools. The office phone rang nonstop as I waited for someone to appear. Finally, a thin and weathered man wearing oil-stained coveralls barged through the door.

"Be right wit-cha," he shouted even though we were only a few feet apart.

"Yello," he hollered into the phone while he perused handwritten notes on a clipboard hung on a nail.

"Yep, we gotcha all ready," he nodded.

"One twenty-eight, yep, that'll do it," he yelled.

"Okee-dokee, yep, ok, yep, see ya then," he said as he slammed the handset onto the base of the phone.

With his back to me, he pulled a cloth hanky out of his pocket and blew his nose with a loud honk before turning around and stuffing the material back into his pocket.

"Howdy, what kin I do fur ya," he said with a brown grin surrounded by patches of hair around his mouth and chin. The name "Lenny" was embroidered on a frayed piece of cloth pinned to his chest.

"I'm looking for someone that worked on a car that broke down a couple of years ago in Charleston," I said.

"My name is Des Campbell and I'm with Legal Aid."

His eyes grew big and his face paled.

"Er you a cop?" he said as he backed up and folded his arms tight across his chest.

"No, no, sir. I'm an attorney... just doing some research," I said.

"There's a stolen car and we're trying to find the owner. It's... well, it's for the wife of a friend," I lied.

"Oh, I see," he said with a sigh and nervous chuckle.

"Do you know if you keep records of all of your service calls?" I asked.

"Sure, yep, we keep 'em all... every one of 'em," he said.

"Would you mind if I..." I began.

"But they ain't here," he interrupted as he pulled at a patch of hair on his face.

"They'd be at Buddy's place in Mount Pleasant. Buddy's the owner," he said with pride.

"Buddy keeps everthin' at his home," he said with wide eyed seriousness as if we were discussing CIA classified material.

"I'd really like to talk to Buddy... do you think I could have that address?" I asked.

"Sure, sure, you betcha," he said, eagerly scribbling a Mount Pleasant address onto the paper side of a chewing gum wrapper.

As I walked up the broken driveway in Mount Pleasant, I felt strangely vulnerable, and I wondered if it wasn't such a good idea to question Buddy alone. The small house was set back from the street in a rural area surrounded by thick forest. Tireless vehicles with missing or cracked windshields were propped on concrete blocks next to a dilapidated two-car garage. Stacks of tires four rows thick bordered the driveway from the garage to the street. The grass grew tall around barrels of metal parts and engines that dotted the secluded property.

I rang the bell and peered into the black window to the right of the small stairs but all I could see was the reflection of ominous clouds in the glass. The rumble of leaves on tree branches filled the air as the storm began to pummel the foliage. I rang the bell again and waited. A howl of wind lifted a milk carton funnel onto the concrete driveway, and I jerked as the container scraped the length of it before tumbling onto the grass.

I thought of leaving right then and there, but like the horror movie idiot, my curiosity got the best of me. I walked around to the back of the house and just past the first line of trees noticed a man standing over a barrel with billowing smoke and flames protruding above the rim. He wore a sleeveless t-shirt tucked into baggy jeans with a chain connected to a leather pouch stuffed in a back pocket. He stood over the barrel jabbing a rod like instrument as bright orange embers flew into the air and spilled out onto the grass. As I got closer, I could hear angry, vulgar insults as he jabbed over and over at the contents inside the cylinder, kicking at it periodically with the toe of his boot. I stopped and decided to turn back, but then something made him turn around. I was caught.

His gait was fast and aggressive as he barreled his way through the tall weeds towards me with rod in hand. Eyes squinted and jaw clenched, his hand moved to unfasten the snap of a holster that housed what looked like some sort of hunting blade.

"Whatcha sellin' I want none of it," he yelled as he continued to pursue me.

Frozen in my tracks, the "flight" part of "fight or flight" was no longer an option.

Buddy Henry was a big, solid man with dark hair and a deep pitted complexion. He came up to stand directly in front of me. Looking into his dark eyes, I realized he bore a similar description to the man Brandon Thompson encountered at the tracks the day Tessa was killed. Brandon described him as a big man with angry dark eyes and an "ugly" complexion. The hairs on the back of my neck warned me to be afraid. I felt my face pale and my knees buckle. There was something about Buddy Henry that wasn't quite right. Something not quite human and more like a demon hiding in plain sight inside the shell of a man. I started to speak but all I could do was stutter a quiet "ssssorry" to the monster that towered over me.

"Who the hell are ya and what'd ya doin' on ma' paroparty," he shouted.

I swallowed hard and knew I had to think fast if I was going to get out of there in one piece.

"I... uh... my name is... uh... Des, and I... uh, I'm here about a vehicle," I stammered.

My hand trembled as I handed him my business card. He grabbed it from my hand without taking his eyes off me as he peeked quickly at the text on the small card.

"What d' ya wont' hea," he shouted, throwing the card onto the ground and lifting the metal rod slapping it onto the palm of his free hand in succession.

"I'm... I'm looking to find out about a Ford," I said backing up slowly.

"Th-there was an old F-Ford repaired in Charleston a few years back that we think you might have information on," I stuttered.

I contemplated which direction I would run should Buddy decide to lift the rod and strike.

"Lenny said I should come see you," I said.

Buddy seemed to soften a touch when I mentioned Lenny. He studied me for a second before he released the rod with one hand and used it as a cane, leaning on it to support his weight.

"Lenny said you were very meticulous about your paperwork," I said.

"What's met... met-culous," he grunted with suspicious eyes.

"Well, uh, Mr. Henry, Lenny said that you keep very accurate records."

Hoping flattery would work in my favor, I decided to embellish further.

"Lenny is proud to work for you, Mr. Henry. He was sure you could help me," I said.

"Good man, my Lenny," said Buddy as he turned to spit a glob of chewing tobacco onto the grass behind him. He wiped his mouth with the back of his hand and continued.

"Lenny... he a good boy... a good boy, I tell ya. I tell 'em eat dirt and he do it," said Buddy with a boastful grin revealing two black spaces where teeth once sat.

"I git him out-ta jail and git 'em a job," said Buddy as he rested one hand on his hip perusing the junkyard.

"He git a little rough with the ex is all," he said with a menacing chuckle.

"They all whores... ever last one of 'em," he said again turning to look at me and chuckling with the assumption that I shared an appreciation of his humor. I thought about what "rough" meant to Buddy Henry and I felt a tinge of nausea.

"They sure are," I said going along with him in order to hopefully, get out of there alive.

"So, about that paperwork," I said.

"It's in tha' house," he said motioning for me to follow him. I walked behind Buddy with trepidation through the backyard around piles of old metal and debris as we made our way to the house. My car sat parked only a few yards away. With a good sprint, I could easily get to it. I reached inside my jacket to feel for my keys as I contemplated running. My better judgment told me to get out of there as fast as I could, but Buddy was the only one with the information I needed. I had to get what I came for.

Buddy pushed open the door to the dark house and turned on a dim light in the small living room. Blue wax drifted lazily inside a Lava Lamp that illuminated a corner of the room. The shock of what I saw next frightened me more than the threat of his fist. Taped to each wall were hardcore pornographic posters of young women in various poses. Stacks of Hustler and other smut magazines were piled on top of tables. There were empty beer bottles and food containers strewn over furniture and floors. Walls were dingy and some had holes from which I imagined an angry fist may have penetrated. Dirty dishes were piled in the sink and on countertops. There was not an inch of clean, clutter free space in the house. I felt filthy just being there and couldn't wait to get out.

"Don't mind the mess... maid's off ta-day," Buddy chuckled before he spit into an old tin cup he kept on a windowsill. In a back bedroom were file cabinets stacked on all four sides of the room and piles of papers in cardboard boxes in the middle of the floor. A metal desk coated with dust sat in one corner of the room with a reading lamp and stacks of papers on top of it.

"Let's see here," he said.

"We is gonna have to charge ya fur all this, he said, looking at me with one raised brow.

"Of course," I said nodding.

A rush of rain beat against the window and thunder roared steadily in the background. If I told him my car windows were open, I could easily make a run for it. Keenly aware of Buddy's erratic temperament, I kept myself positioned close to the door just in case.

"The ex did a poor job of fi-lin," he said.

"Good fer nothing... nasty whore," he shouted sending drops of spit into the air.

"Dun nothin' but spend my money... all she done," he screamed.

Buddy went into a tyrannical rage spewing insults and hateful threats against his ex for a full minute while I kept a sharp eye on his every move. I could feel my palms start to sweat inside the pockets of my jacket. Buddy was oblivious to my presence until after he finished his rant. He exhibited all the characteristics of a psycho killer, and in particular, the kind that hated women. Buddy scratched his head and sat down on a wheeled stool and began perusing duct tape labels on the drawers of the file cabinets.

"Now what year did ya say you's lookin' fer," he said calmly as if I hadn't just witnessed him losing his mind.

"That would be July 4... 1967," I said.

Buddy crab crawled his way over to a metal cabinet near the corner of the room and yanked at the bottom drawer of the rusted shell.

"Let's see..." he said as he thumbed through handwritten tabs on worn file folders.

"'Ere she is," he said, pulling out a folder covered in black fingerprints to peruse the documents inside.

Buddy mumbled to himself as he turned page after page.

"Yep, nope, no, no, no, yep," he said with squinted eyes as he struggled to read in the dim light of a single bulb that swayed overhead.

"Got cha, right cheer," he said holding the file tight to his person.

"That'll be fifty dollars," he said with a Grinch-like smirk.

"Fi... fifty?" I choked.

This was an outrageous amount of money, but I had no choice. I would pay him, get what I came for and get out of there.

"Ok," I said reaching for my back pocket hoping I had enough money to appease his greed.

I opened my wallet and pulled out everything I had and counted.

"Five, five, ten and five one's... twenty-five," I said nervously.

"I only have twenty-five, but I can get the rest to you tomorrow."

"Check yer pockets," he said impatiently.

"You's might have more in yer pockets," he shouted with agitation.

I reached into the pockets of my trousers pulling out the white material on each side of my pants like rabbit ears.

"I'm sorry... it's all I have," I said.

Annoyed, Buddy stood to his feet and paced in the small space. I could see the wheels turning as he scratched at his arms and neck. He looked at the twenty-five dollars and without warning, grabbed the money out of my hand quickly like the lizard's tongue snatching its prey. With a sly smile, he extended his arm to hand me the file, but then quickly pulled it back as I reached for it.

"Not so fast," he teased.

"Give us a look at cher time piece, there," he said motioning to my wrist.

On my right wrist was a gold watch Jean had given me on a Christmas morning. I wasn't particularly fond of the style, preferring a simpler design, but it was a reliable watch that I wore regularly. I unfastened the clasp with a sigh and handed over the gold-plated watch to Buddy. He immediately placed it on his wrist and stretched out his arm in a rather feminine posture to admire his thick wrist.

"I'll take it," he said before we even had a deal.

He shoved the file at me, and I quickly tucked it into my pocket as he continued to study the detail in the gold band.

With a quick "thank you," I sprinted to the front door and got out of there as fast as I could.

Half-way to my car I heard the front door open.

"Time piece is a piece of garbage, like you is... little sissy faggot," he shouted as he made his way towards my vehicle. I jumped into my car and locked the doors, fumbling for my key and jamming it into the ignition. He reached the driver's window as I pulled the drive shift to "D" and stepped hard on the gas pedal. My tires squealed on the pavement as I pulled onto the dark road, my heart racing out of my chest.

THE WRINKLED receipt was faded and oil stained, but the vehicle type and date were clear. The1959 Ford Galaxie was serviced on July 4, 1967, at 12:35pm. I strained to read the customer signature at the bottom of the paper and what looked like "Kat or Kit Nolan."

"I'm not sure," I said handing the paper to Donny.

Donny held the magnifying glass over the receipt carefully tracing the dim curved strokes one at a time. He grumbled under his breath before handing over the document to Leah and reaching for another slice of pizza. Leah glanced at the signature for only a moment.

"It's Kit and the last name is Moran," she said.

Donny and I both stopped chewing at the same time and looked to one another in bewilderment.

"Are you sure?" we said in unison.

"Of course, I'm sure," she said sharply as she went to the stroller to remove the pacifier from Christopher's mouth while he slept.

Donny grabbed the paper and we both studied it some more.

"Yep... I think she's right," he said. It looks like Kit Moran."

We immediately grabbed the thick phone book and began searching through the Moran's.

"There's no Kit," I said pushing the book away in frustration.

"Just hold on," said Donny.

"Maybe it's a nickname for Kevin or Keith," he said.

"We'll make a list and run them through the C.P.D. database for a match."

Our plan was to revisit evidence previously denied at trial and focus on two details that could potentially exonerate Brandon Thompson and lead us to the real killer. But first, we needed to uncover the owner of the Ford that was used to deliver flowers to Tessa. Second, the stranger in the woods needed to be identified. Somewhere in the back of my mind something told me they were one in the same.

Twenty

Jean tossed and turned for two hours before reaching for the small alarm clock. It was nearly midnight. She lay wide awake even though she had worn herself to the brink of exhaustion. She had tended to the rose bushes in the hot sun the entire day. Later, she soaked in a warm tub and then nurtured the tiny cuts on her fingers and hands with the sap from an Aloe Vera plant. It's not that she couldn't have had one of the stable hands care for the shrubs, but she loved the roses and took great pride in the generous blooms and deep rich colors her toil produced.

It was the third time this week he was gone from morning till night and Jean was beginning to suspect he was involved with another woman.

Again. Jean had had her suspicions before but that was when she was young and naïve. Back then she would convince herself his absence was due to the demands of the job. He would tell her the long hours were a sacrifice for the family, for the exquisite house, and the luxuries they all enjoyed. He would raise his thunderous voice and shut down even the smallest hint of complaint with dominant force. Now, at fifty-two, she had grown tired of the long nights alone. She was tired of making excuses for a marriage void of affection and meaning. She no longer cared about being the wife of a high-profile attorney and the prestige associated with it. After Des went away to college, there was nothing left. The large home began to feel more and more empty and as did the union with Rudy. Jean began to take solace in her faith. She finally felt strong enough to share her feelings with a man she truly trusted, Pastor John Templeton.

Jean met with Pastor John on a rainy afternoon in June. John had had his suspicions of Jean's troubled marriage long ago. Rumors circulated throughout the community over the years of Rudy Campbell's infidelities. That as well as Jean's solo church attendance hinted that the marriage was frail. John Templeton had never married even though he had been proposed to twice. He had a girlfriend or two before entering the Seminary, but after college, he had immersed himself in the church which had grown into a congregation of more than three hundred members. John always found time for those who needed his help and Jean was more than just a member of the church, she was a close friend.

"Hi John," said Jean, reaching out to shake his hand.

"Hello there, come in before you get washed away," said John with a chuckle, taking Jean's umbrella and tapping it several times on the braided rug before setting it in the corner of the small office.

She handed John her raincoat and then sat down at the small table while John prepared two cups of Orange Peko Tea. Sensing all was not well John was careful to stifle his normal jovial side in favor of the kind sensitivity the congregation admired and depended on. With creased brow, she looked down at her clasped hands rubbing her thumbs one over the other repeatedly.

"Here you, go," said John with a fatherly tenderness as he set the teacup and saucer in front of her. He sat down and reached for her hand and that's when the tears came as heavy as the deluge of rain on the window.

"There now, Jean," John said, cupping her hand in both of his.

"I'm so sorry, John," she said in between gasps of air.

She traced her lower lids with the tips of her fingers careful to avoid smudging the mascara on her eyelashes. John reached for a box of Kleenex and set it on the table.

"Thank you, John. You're so kind," she said.

"I haven't done anything yet," he joked.

Jean looked at John and smiled for the first time. A sad smile, but it was better than nothing.

"You know, I thought I did good, John. I thought I picked someone that would take care of me and my children," she said as she dabbed her eyes with a tissue.

"He was hard working and ambitious," she cried.

"I admired that, you know," she said as tears again streamed down her cheeks.

Jean was still a beautiful woman. A classic beauty. The Grace Kelly kind of pretty with wavy satin curls, a petite frame and striking gray eyes. John listened intently as she spoke. It was nothing he hadn't heard before, but this one got to him more than the others. Jean was genuinely good, and she deserved better. Why does she stay? he thought as he studied the curve of her face and the tiny lines that cascaded from the corners of her eyes. John wished he could say what he truly felt, but it was his obligation to try and save marriages, not end them. They talked for a full hour as the rain stopped and orange rays of sun poked through the remaining clouds.

"Thank you, John," she said as she buttoned up her coat.

With a quick hug, she made her way down the wet sidewalk. Wishing she could stay longer, he sighed and watched her as she turned the corner and disappeared.

Twenty-one

Ray Combs ran a search for the Ford, but it only revealed two Moran's with first names that began with a "K." One of the Moran's was a paraplegic that lived on a small farm on Johns Island. Ken Moran was mangled inside a Combine Harvester shortly after he purchased the Ford. His wife confirmed the accident happened two years before Tessa's murder. After that, the car was repossessed for lack of payment and resold to a college student from Tennessee named Roger Dalton. The other "K" was a young woman named Karly Moran who boarded an Appaloosa at Deerwood Stables in Aiken. Both the Moran's had no connection to Tessa Rhodes, and both had solid alibis.

"I'll continue to search," said Ray.

"If there's anything at all that hints of a possibility, I'll be sure to dig."

Des, doubting the owner of the Ford would turn up, hung up the phone in frustration. Des and Brenner both solemn, sat in the quiet office contemplating their next move.

"Maybe whoever signed the receipt isn't the owner of the vehicle," said Des.

"Maybe the car was borrowed, and we need to direct our focus to the stranger in the woods," he said. "Right," said Donny now staring blankly out the window.

"Let's talk to Brandon Thompson again," said Des.

"Maybe there's something more. Maybe there's something he forgot," he said.

WE DROVE to Lee Correctional Institute early on Saturday morning. Leah, angry I was spending another Saturday working, turned away when I bent to kiss her goodbye. All my time over the past several months was dedicated to the Thompson case. I guess you could say it had become an obsession. I knew it was taking its toll on my family, but I couldn't stop now. We were so close. We drove through a small dusty town and stopped at a diner just a mile from the federal prison. A sea of eyes followed me as I made my way to the payphone near the front entrance of the small canteen.

"Hello," she said.

"Leah, it's me," I said.

She hung up the phone before I could speak, and I stood there like an idiot in the quiet room.

"Damn it," I said as I slammed the receiver down hard on the handset and turned around to a row of faces on barstools staring back at me.

"Good morning," I said with a tart smirk to the looky-loos.

They stared hard and I stared back. Their suspicious eyes followed me as I made my way through the greasy diner back to our table.

"How's she doing?" said Ray.

"She's fine," I lied.

"She's busy with the baby," I said quietly.

Ray and Donny could see right through me. They knew there was trouble at home but didn't push and I was grateful because I would have bit their heads off. We finished our coffee without speaking and paid our bill.

"You boys look about as happy as sailors in a raft," said the jovial waitress with a red bee-hive hairdo.

She looked to be in her mid-forties, and I thought she must have spent her whole life working in the diner. She seemed a part of it like a fixture that somehow belonged there.

"Thank you, ma'am," said Donny.

"You took good care of us," he said handing her a generous five-dollar tip.

"Well now, you make sure you come back and see us a-gin," she said with a flirtatious wink. Her smile never waned as she tucked the five deep inside her bosom and watched us exit the diner.

We went through the usual routine at Lee Correctional but this time the Corrections Officers took it easy on us most likely because Ray was with us. The visitors' area was full, so we were escorted to Brandon's cell. Walking through the living quarters of the prison gave us full view of life at L.C.I. It was bad... horrible really. Inmates jeered and made vulgar gestures as we walked through the concrete dormitory. The roar of voices was deafening and intimidating. We were advised not to look at them, but I couldn't help it. Like rabid animals, they preyed on anything that moved outside their cells. The C.O. periodically slapped a metal baton on the bars when an inmate was especially rude.

"Shut your filthy mouth," he screamed as he slammed the baton on a bar narrowly missing a row of fingers. We were dead men if a breach in security were to occur, so from that moment on, I kept my eyes low for fear of agitating the already volatile mob.

Brandon's cell was at the end of a row on the third and highest level of the facility. It was still noisy but at least we could hear one another. The C.O. opened the cell door, warning Brandon with an ominous glare. He pulled a hanky from his pocket and let out a phlegmy cough and then spit out a glob in the corner of the small cell.

"You have a half hour," said the C.O., wiping his mouth with the hanky.

"I'll be right over there," he said pointing towards the end of the hallway.

"If he gives you trouble, use the whistle," he said, handing a large silver whistle to Ray.

Ray took the whistle and stuffed it in the pocket of his trousers. Brandon, sitting on a corner of the bed had been assaulted. Whoever it was that hurt him had done so freely. His right eye was nearly swollen shut and under his lower lip was a deep open gash. He had trouble sitting in one position for more than a few minutes, shifting his weight from one side to the other repeatedly. Each time he did that he winced and closed his eyes for a second or two. It appeared that fighting for his life was a regular routine. I felt sorry for him. Ray was used to these types of situations, so he spoke first.

"Hi Brandon, how've you been," said Ray.

Brandon nodded and shrugged his shoulders. I looked around at the stark cell. There was a small rusty toilet in the corner and a child-size sink mounted to the wall. His bed was a thin soiled mattress and a small wool blanket that barely covered the length of it. A Bible and some tattered copies of National Geographic Magazine were the only reading materials. Based on his condition, I wondered if Brandon could read at all. The bare walls were a yellowish white except for patches of red paint where the white paint had flaked and scattered in tiny chips on the dank floor. The only glimmer of hope was a crumpled piece of colorful artwork taped to the wall at the starboard side of the small cell.

"Brandon, you remember Des Campbell, and this is Don Brenner," said Ray.

"We want to talk again about the day you were at the tracks."

"Now, I know you said that..." said Ray.

"I don't know any more," said Brandon quickly.

"I know, I understand," said Ray cautiously.

"But we really need you to take us through that day one more time. Slowly, please Brandon. Sometimes there are things you remember later on, even years later," he said.

Brandon sighed and looked down at his hands before he spoke.

"I was at the tracks early, almost 11:00am," he said.

"I brought all the paint with me, and I found a good place."

I didn't know what he was talking about paint and a good place, but I didn't want to interrupt. He never mentioned that to me the last time we spoke.

"I sprayed the boxcar most of the day," he said.

"How long were you tagging, Brandon?" said Ray.

"Most of the day, cause when I got to T. Park, the tower clock said almost 2:30pm," said Brandon.

"I finished the whole thing and when I was done, I heard something," he said.

"It sounded like a woman, like a scream or a laugh…. close by."

"I was scared F.R.A. were going to catch me tagging, so I threw paint cans in the car and took off through the woods," he said.

"I was running fast and then turned back because I heard something behind me and... I ran right into him!"

"He was big and mean looking... angry," he said.

"Tell us again what he looked like, Brandon," said Ray.

"Ummm... dark hair, big, dark eyes, holes in his skin," he said touching his right cheek lightly with his fingers.

"He had a funny mark on his arm," he said as Donny nearly jumped out of his skin.

"What!" shouted Donny.

Startled, Brandon jumped back and stopped talking as Ray turned to Donny with a sharp grimace.

"Brandon, what kind of funny mark?"

"Please continue," said Ray.

"It... it was round with things coming out of it. It was a brownish color," said Brandon.

"On the arm... that one," he said pointing to Ray's right arm.

"Are you sure?" said Ray as he moved in closer to Brandon.

"I'm sure," said Brandon.

"Was it ink or more like a birthmark? Try and remember, Brandon," said Ray.

"Easy does it, Ray. Give him time!" said Donny.

"I don't know. I don't know," said Brandon shaking his head.

Brandon's explanation was confusing, but he tried his best to describe the mark and its location on the arm. Finally, we pulled the artwork from the wall and used the backside to let him draw what he couldn't describe. The image was the size of a quarter and looked like the sun with jagged rays protruding from its perimeter. We surmised it might be a large birth mark or tattoo etched on the stranger's right arm just below the bend of the elbow.

"Times up," said the C.O.

"You did good. Real good," said Ray.

"We'll be in touch," said Donny as we exited the cell and made our way out.

Twenty-two

We took Christopher to Jean and Rudy's for the night. I didn't much like leaving him there, but Leah and I were desperate for some quality time alone. It was a Friday night and Jean was thrilled to have Christopher all to herself. Leah, on the other hand, was aloof and quiet all the way to the restaurant. We were seated at a nice table in the corner of our favorite Italian place. She wasn't saying much, and my mind kept drifting to Brandon. Something about our meeting was nagging at me, but I couldn't figure it out.

"How's your dinner?" I asked.

"Good, it's good," she said quietly.

"I wanted to say a few things, Leah. I know you haven't been happy, but I want to explain."

Just then the waiter appeared and poured more wine. It seemed every time I was about to speak, we were interrupted by the overzealous wait staff.

"I, well you know I want to spend time with you and Christopher," I said.

She looked at me with a blank stare and I began to feel angry but held back.

"The Thompson case... it's almost over. We have to get it right. We only have one shot at it—just one," I said hoping for a glimmer of empathy.

"You know, our son is only one year old once. Only once, and we have to get that right," she said sharply.

"I only ask for the weekends," she said.

"I know, but you don't understand," I pleaded.

"*I* don't understand!?" she said loudly.

Our waiter began to approach but then quietly retreated behind a wall.

A subtle tenseness lingered for the rest of the evening, but we managed to make it through the night without another argument. When we got into bed, I pulled Leah close, and we held one another tight even though our thoughts were miles apart. She drifted off to sleep and an hour later and still restless, I got up and headed to the kitchen. I pulled the paper from Brandon's cell out of my briefcase and studied it carefully under the kitchen light. It looked like a homemade tattoo of a sun, the rays of which appeared jagged or perhaps the tattoo had bled over the years. I turned the paper over to peruse the colorful drawing on the flip side. I felt like I had seen it somewhere before, but my mind was foggy, and between Brandon and Leah, nothing was making sense.

In the morning, we drove to the mansion to pick up Christopher.

"Hello," I said as we entered the large foyer.

The home was unnaturally quiet.

"Hello, anybody home?" I said again as we walked through the hallway and into the kitchen.

"Where could they be?" Leah said as we entered the large kitchen.

"I don't know."

We walked back to the foyer stopping to investigate each of the large rooms along the way but still no sign of anyone. I raced up the stairs to the bedrooms and checked each one, but they were all empty.

Leah stood at the bottom of the stairs looking up at me with worry in her eyes.

"Don't panic," I said.

I grabbed her hand, and we exited the house toward the stable. It was just then we heard a child's shriek, and we froze. We immediately raced into the stable past the horse stalls and then outside to the corral. At the far end of the corral, we saw a small figure sitting on top of a pony. Rudy was there along with Kendall and a few of the stable hands.

"He loves it!" shouted Rudy as we approached the group.

Christopher shrieked again when he saw Leah.

"How are you, Desmond?" said Rudy.

"Where'd you get the pony?" I asked.

"Your mother wanted to surprise Christopher with something special," he said.

"We bought him from a farmer in West Ashley. He was in rough shape when we got him."

"Kendall's friend here, Wes Hampton is a farrier and fixed the little guy."

We watched Christopher as he squealed atop the small Shetland. It was good to see Leah smiling again.

"How long have you been tending horses, Wes?" I asked.

"About as long as I can remember," he said adjusting the Stetson that sat atop his weathered face.

"I'd say just as long as Kit and I been friends," he said.

"Who?" I asked.

"Kit," said Wes as he gestured with his chin toward Kendall Morgan.

I was confused as I had never heard the name "Kit." It didn't sink in at first, but then it hit me like a Freight Train, and I began to feel nauseous and disoriented.

Wes opened a small cylinder, plucked a thick pinch of dark moss and tucked it down behind his lower lip causing it to jut awkwardly. Kendall turned to Wes with a subtle acknowledgement and lifted his arm bringing the remnant of a small cigar to his lips. And that's when I saw it. The small brown sphere the size of a quarter with jagged beams that protruded from its perimeter. Why hadn't I noticed it before? There it was below the crease of the elbow just like Brandon had described. My head started spinning and I felt as though I was sinking into the ground. I turned to face Kendall directly. His dark eyes penetrated deep into mine, the same soulless gaze I had witnessed with the death of his only child, Leslie. My hands trembled and my heart raced out of control. It was him! It was Kendall Morgan at the tracks the day Tessa was killed! I couldn't speak as I was consumed with the realization the real killer had been in plain sight the whole time. My mind raced to Donna Page and the description of the strange man that visited the shop repeatedly. The odd behavior, average looks and ruddy complexion all matched Kendall Morgan to a 'T'. Brandon's recollection of a big man with mean, dark eyes and a distinct mark on the skin. The tattoo with jagged lines protruding from the center located exactly where Brandon said it was on the man's right arm. I thought about Rudy's flirtatious demeanor with Tessa Rhodes and how uncomfortable he made her when she interviewed him for the school paper. I remembered the roses from Page's Floristry that were sent to us after Christopher was born. The same florist where all the other anonymous bouquets were purchased and left on the Rhodes' doorstep. I thought about Tessa and how she was kind, fearless and full of life. How she saw the good in everyone, but mostly I thought about how she died and how terrified she must have been. I recounted the photographs and the brutality of her death, the purple marks left on her skin and neck. Her blood red eyes would forever taint my memory of her and how it filled me with rage. It all made sense now. All of the puzzle pieces fit together, and the realization that Kendall was the killer made me sick to the point I felt I would vomit right then and there. My head was spinning as I stumbled toward the center of the corral. Instinctively, I lunged for Christopher and pulled him from the saddle.

"We have to go!" I snapped.

"What?" asked Leah.

"What are you doing!" she shouted.

"Leah, we have to go!" I yelled.

"What's wrong with you, he's having fun!" she screamed.

I thrust Christopher off the pony as he began to wail and raced to the car without stopping.

"I'm sorry!" said Leah to Jean with angry eyes.

We buckled Christopher in the car seat while he cried, and I sped away as fast as I could.

"What is wrong with you! He was having fun!" she screamed with tears that ran freely as Christopher's cry grew increasingly louder.

"Now look what you've done!" she yelled.

When we were far enough away, I spotted a phonebooth and pulled over. Leah jumped out of the car and opened the rear door to console Christopher and make up for the damage I had done. When I got back to the car, Christopher, quieted by a pacifier, watched us through tear-stained eyes as Leah stared out the side window.

"It's him," I said in heavy breaths.

"What?" she asked.

"The man at the tracks the day Tessa was killed... it was Kendall Morgan!"

"Are you sure?!" she asked.

"Yes, yes, it's him," I said as my voice quaked.

It's him!" I shouted.

I sped through Charleston with my hands clutching the steering wheel.

Brenner raced into the office and Ray arrived shortly thereafter. Leah rocked Christopher in the stroller while we reviewed the new evidence. I reached for the file from Buddy's Towing to reexamine the receipts.

"Wait! Why didn't I see it before?" I said with both hands resting on top of my head.

"Look!" I said as I pulled out the towing receipts and laid them out over the table.

"The signatures! Look at the signatures! They all have a crease where the third letter is supposed to be."

"There must have been a depression in a clipboard or whatever they used to hold the receipts," I said.

Donny and Ray quietly studied the documents one by one.

"He's right," said Donny slowly.

"The signature for "Kit Moran" is missing the 'G,' he said.

"It's Morgan... it's Kit Morgan not Moran," said Ray.

"Look at this one! It's supposed to be Matthews, not Mathews," I said.

"But why? Why would Kendall do it? It doesn't make any sense, un... unless" I said slowly.

"Unless what?" said Brenner.

"Rudy," I said solemnly.

Somehow, I felt Rudy had to be involved, but I didn't know for sure.

DONNY AND I went to work right away on the Motions for New Trial. We would challenge the conviction and prove the new evidence would exonerate Brandon Thompson. We would also argue that the legal team failed to provide Brandon with adequate counsel. We knew the Motion would have to be compelling and flawless, so we worked day and night preparing the documents to the point we were both sick and tired of reviewing them. After that, we hired outside counsel for additional scrutiny. Finally, after seven weeks, we were confident the Motion was ready. Melanie submitted the documents to the court, and we waited.

Four weeks later we received a notice.

"It's here! It's here!" said Melanie as she raced down the narrow hallway.

Donny couldn't get the envelope open fast enough.

"What is it? What does it say!" I yelled.

"Hold on" he said as he raised one hand while scanning the letter.

"Damn it," he whispered.

"Damn it! We're denied," he said tossing the letter on the desktop.

"What!" I yelled.

"How can they do that!?" I cried.

"They can do it. But we can appeal. We just have to work a little harder," he said.

But how could I? Leah and I were barely speaking to each other as it was.

I decided to visit Page's Floristry and plead for help. Donna was just locking up the shop door when I came up close behind her. She quickly turned and then jumped covering her chest with one hand.

"I'm sorry, I didn't mean to scare you," I said.

"Oh goodness! I wasn't expecting anyone to be there!" she said.

"How are you, Des," she said while she fanned herself with an envelope.

"This is Ted, he's the newest member of our family," I said reaching down to stroke the back of a Golden Labrador we rescued from the local shelter.

"Oh, he's just beautiful! Gorgeous!" she said stooping to stroke his head.

"Congratulations. He's a beauty," she said.

"Donna, I need a favor. Um... another favor," I said sheepishly.

"Donna, you're the daughter of the late governor, right?" I asked.

"Yes, that's right."

"Well, we're having some trouble securing the new trial," I said.

"We have new evidence that could turn this thing upside down, but the court denied us."

"If your father, was a friend of Judge Phillips, perhaps he would listen to you," I pleaded.

"I don't know, Des," she said, shaking her head.

"He was friends with Judge Phillips, but my father and I were estranged for many years and then he passed."

"I know my father cared for me, but we just could never see eye to eye," she said.

"Everyone that knew him was aware of our relationship."

"But could you just ask?" I pleaded.

"If you ask, maybe, just maybe, he will reconsider."

"I just don't know if Brandon Thompson can survive in L.C.I much longer" I said.

Donna studied me for a minute and frowned as she thought about what I said.

"I don't think I could. I'm sorry, Des," she said as she dropped her envelope into the mailbox.

"I don't like it that a young boy like that may be wrongly incarcerated, but I don't think I can help."

"Good luck, Des," she said with a squeeze of my arm.

"Ok, I understand," I said even though I didn't.

DONNY AND I submitted the appeal and waited. It was nearly seven weeks, and we still hadn't heard anything. I sat at my desk on a rainy Monday afternoon shooting rubber bands at random targets and wondered what we would do if they denied us again. How would we tell Brandon we had failed? If he didn't get out of Lee Correctional soon, he may not make it out alive. I thought about Tessa Rhodes, her parents, Brenner and Ray Combs. I thought about Leah and Christopher mostly and about Kendall Morgan and the monster that lurked inside him. The office was especially quiet today, and I jumped when the phone rang.

"Hello," I said.

"Yes, this is Des Campbell. What? Really?! It's been granted?! Are you sure?" I said jumping to my feet.

"Great! This is great! Thank you, yes, yes, thank you. That's great news," I said. I ran to Donny's office half tripping and flung open the door.

"We got it!" I shouted.

"What?!" he said.

"The court just called! We got it!" I said jumping up and down.

"Yes! Thank you, Jesus," Donny said with his head in his hands.

Melanie joined us in the small office, and we celebrated but only briefly. The real work was yet to come. We had only five weeks to prepare for the trial. Charleston Police Department under new leadership gave Ray Combs the greenlight to revisit the Thompson case. Donny, Ray, Melanie and I worked around the clock preparing while Ray took statements from witnesses including Kendall Morgan. Based on testimony, we were able to piece together the crime and the timeline. We would argue Kendall Morgan delivered the flowers to Tessa Rhodes the afternoon of July 4, 1967. He was the last person to see Tessa alive and he could be identified as being at the crime scene. The motive, however, was still a mystery.

Ray Combs studied Kendall Morgan through the one-way glass window in the interrogation room.

He paces, doesn't ask why he's being brought in for questioning and can't vouch for his whereabouts the afternoon Tessa is killed. Ray and colleague, Jim Bartholomew take statements from Kendall methodically befriending him and trapping him in several lies.

"I worked all day in the stable," he said with darting eyes that bounce between Jim and Ray.

"So, you didn't go anywhere and didn't leave the mansion on July 4, 1967?" said Jim.

"No," said Kendall unmoving.

"We have evidence from four sources that say you did, said Combs, quietly as Kendall shifts in his chair and beads of sweat form across his brow.

"We know you left the stable that morning and we know you didn't return until after 5pm," said Jim.

"No!" said Kendall who begins scratching his arms.

"We have a receipt right here from Buddy's Towing with your signature on it... Kit," said Combs as he holds up the receipt.

Kendall's eyes flash when he hears the name Kit. He doesn't crack but they can see he's getting angry. 'Gotcha', thought Combs as he continued.

"We know you were at Page's Floristry the morning Tessa Rhodes was killed. The same way we know you had car trouble and used Buddy's to fix the car," said Combs leaning in close to Kendall.

"We also think you drove to the Rhodes' house after that."

But, that wasn't the first time, was it, Kit?" said Combs.

"We know there was shards of glass and buds from a rose on the Rhodes' porch near the unlocked front door," said Combs.

"We also know you ran into a young boy in the woods just a few yards from where Tessa Rhodes' body was found," said Jim.

"No!" shouted Kendall shaking his head, now covered in sweat and beat red.

Combs waits and lets the tension build in the quiet room.

"And finally, we know you took her from her home and dumped her under a Willow tree at the tracks," said Combs cutting through Kendall like a knife.

"No! I need a phone," says Kendall with trembling hands.

Combs and Jim leave the room and allow Kendall to use the phone on the desk while they listen from a nearby room. He calls Rudy.

They now have evidence to support the theory that Kendall Morgan killed Tessa Rhodes. The boy in the stable, now a young man, also proved a good witness and recounted the day Kendall Morgan left the mansion for several hours.

"Yes, I remember," said Billy Hamilton.

"He left the stable a few minutes after I started my shift and didn't come back till I was fixin' to leave around five."

"Did you see him or talk to him when he arrived back at the mansion," said Jim.

"Yes, I saw him. I was sitting on a bench changing my shoes and he walked right into the stable right in front of me, but he didn't say a word. He looked sort of in a trance or something, said Hamilton.

"He was covered in sweat and his arms had scratches with some blood on them. I didn't think much of it at first, but then wondered how he got the scrapes from just being in his car," said Billy shrugging his shoulders.

Ray Combs and I drove to Lee Correctional Institute to prep Brandon for the trial. We had him fitted for a suit and advised him how we anticipated everything would go once we entered the courtroom. We requested Brandon be separated from the other inmates indefinitely so he would be injury free in court. Brandon appeared hopeful for the first time since I'd met him. He stood and reached for my hand.

"Thank you," he said.

Twenty-three

W E BEGAN THE VOIR dire early Monday morning with a group of thirty jurors. Brenner asked the questions and I analyzed. Melanie kept track of the list and juror comments. One by one, we made our selections.

Corey Knowles, white, 57, Democrat, brush cut, retired police officer. *No questions. Strike.*

Martha Bennington, 30, Negro, Democrat, Social Worker, casual dress. "I think everyone deserves a fair and impartial trial, no matter what." *Yes.*

Pastor John Lithgow, 45, Negro, Christian Fellowship Church. "God forgives. Even if you're a murderer." *Mind already made up. Strike.*

Roddy Millsboro, 40, Caucasian, Republican, Conservative, Teacher, frowning. "I look at all the facts, but, personal responsibility is paramount." *Maybe. Noodle on this one.*

Sharon Johansen, 37, white, Republican, President of the Charleston Country Club Women's Group. "I'm not partial to the rich. I hire plenty of poor folk to tend to the grounds of Charleston's Country Club. But they most certainly cannot have a criminal background." *Strike.*

Blake Kepler, 27, white, Republican, son of U.S. Congressman, Southern Charleston. *No questions. Strike*

Karen Mettles, 35, white, Democrat, Community Activist. "Facts. I only care about the facts." *Yes!*

Roger Kowalski, 42, Democrat, white, construction worker, Boys and Girls Club volunteer. "No one should be convicted of any crime without 100% certainty." *Yes*

We knew who we wanted and didn't want and got through the group quickly. Within three days, we had a confirmed list acceptable to both sides and could only hope our due diligence and scrutiny of the jurors was solid. We were ready to go.

PROSECUTION WAS confident in their case against Brandon. Three prosecutors entered the court without acknowledging us and took their seats promptly. Mr. and Mrs. Rhodes sat behind them in the first row along with other relatives and friends of Tessa Rhodes who glared at us continually. Brandon's suit was sloppy, but good enough. He was well groomed and fully counseled.

"Remember," I said as he sat down between Brenner and me.

"Don't look to your right or left. Don't turn around. Just keep your eyes forward," I whispered.

"Stick to what we talked about," I said.

Brandon nodded even though it was clear he was a nervous wreck. We all were. The witnesses would be called exactly as planned. We wouldn't push any of them further than we had to so as not to instigate the judge or jury. We were the underdogs. We needed to mind our manners, trust the process and stick to our strategy.

Prosecution began with Brandon's criminal record.

"Ladies and gentlemen, we will prove... once again.." said Bob Lipp, lead prosecutor.

"That the young man sitting right there," said Bob pointing directly at Brandon.

"Brandon Michael Thompson is guilty of the murder of Tessa Rhodes. We will prove he was at the crime scene the day Tessa was killed. We will also provide evidence that Mr. Thompson lied about where he was on that day." he said.

"We will prove that Mr. Thompson lied about knowing Tessa Rhodes. The motive for the murder, ladies and gentlemen," he said standing directly in front of the jury, "*rejection!*"

Brandon's reaction was swift.

"He lied!" said Brandon in a loud whisper.

I motioned to him to remain calm.

"Remember what I said... don't react," I whispered.

He relented and settled back in his chair though he was shaken. Prosecution continued their defamation of Brandon's character for a full twenty-five minutes as Brandon grew more agitated. The stress of the trial as well as his physical ailments made it uncomfortable for him to sit for long periods of time. Brandon had been isolated in Lee Correctional Institute for a good deal of time throughout the four years. Taking him out of that environment and into a courtroom was overwhelming. Underneath his hard exterior, Brandon was shy, quiet and scared.

"Hang in there," I whispered to him as I rose to begin opening statement.

"Ladies and gentlemen," I began. We intend to prove that Brandon Michael Thompson is not a murderer," I said directly to the jurors.

"We will prove well beyond a reasonable doubt that Brandon Thompson is not only innocent, but that it was impossible for him to commit the crime he's accused of. The only crime Brandon Thompson is guilty of is theft," I said.

"Brandon is guilty of stealing spray paint from the local five and dime."

"Now we're not arguing that stealing is not worth a punishment," I said.

"It most certainly is. However, Brandon is not a murderer, and he did not kill Tessa Rhodes," I said looking at each juror one by one.

"Brandon Thompson is an artist. You heard that right. He's an artist and he stole spray paint to paint murals on the boxcars. I intend to prove that Brandon Thompson was at the railroad tracks tagging at the exact time Tessa Rhodes was killed at her home. I also intend to present to you another individual who was in the woods by the tracks the day Tessa Rhodes was killed... near to where her body was found.

"We believe, ladies and gentlemen, that the new evidence I am about to present will exonerate my client, Brandon Thompson."

I finished opening statement and felt like we had a good start. We broke for fifteen minutes and then the judge called a motion to adjourn to the following day based on one of the jurors falling ill.

Court resumed early Monday morning. The judge, apparently having overslept, kept us waiting for well over an hour. Brandon was a basket case, drinking nearly an entire picture of water while we waited.

"Let's hope he's awake when he finally shows up," said Brenner.

I escorted Brandon to the latrine for the second time and waited in the hallway. Mr. Rhodes entered the latrine just as Brandon was exiting. He looked as haggard and thin as ever. His dark eyes pierced us as tangible anger seeped through every pore on his frail body.

"Burn in hell," he said through clenched teeth.

Brandon was rattled. I grabbed his arm and quickly pulled him away from Rhodes who continued to spout insults as we made our way down the long hall back to court. The judge was now seated and looked annoyed.

"Glad you could join us," he grumbled as we sat down. Brandon's hands trembled under the table.

"Don't pay him no mind. He's been miserable since the day he was born," said Donny with a wink.

Robert Lipp, lead prosecutor started. The first witness called to the stand was Laura Knolls. Laura and her daughter, Peg were at the street parade the day Brandon ran through the crowd.

"He come runnin' from the woods," said Laura.

"Is the person you saw running from the woods, in this room?" said Lipp.

"Why yes. He's right there," she said pointing directly at Brandon.

"I remember it just like it's yesterday. The poor girl."

"In your opinion, what emotional state do you think the defendant was in?" said Lipp.

"Objection."

"Sustained," said the judge.

"You will rephrase the question."

"In your opinion, Mrs. Knolls, how did the defendant look when you saw him running out of the woods?" said Lipp.

"Panic! Why he looked like he was in a panic," she said wide eyed.

"Like he done somethin'," said Laura.

"Objection."

"Sustained. The court will ignore Ms. Knolls' opinion," Judge said sharply.

"Your witness," said Lipp.

I approached the witness with a smile and thanked Laura for her service to the court. She seemed to like that, and relaxed.

"Laura, have you ever feared something that maybe other people thought you shouldn't be so scared of?"

"Well yes, I guess I could say that I have," she said.

"Can you give me an example of that…something that scared you that other people thought may be silly?"

"Well, let me see here," she said reminiscing.

"Why yes! Well, this is quite funny now, you know, but wasn't so funny then," she said with a nervous giggle.

"You see I's at the Five and Dime down over Baker Square, and I'd gone into the store for some apples. It was my husband's 50th birthday and I figured I'd make his favorite... apple crumb pie," she said.

"Objection," shouted prosecution.

"Where are we going with this?"

"Are we going somewhere with this?" asked the Judge with a frustrated sigh.

"Yes, yes we are, your honor," I stammered.

"Overruled. Hurry up, Mr. Campbell," said the Judge.

"Go ahead, please Laura."

"Well, you see I's in the Five and Dime like I said, and I was in the produce section of the store looking for some apples and as I's scanning over the pile, I saw the most beautiful red apples you ever seen. So, I grabbed up a bag and started filling it up and just as I's about to reach for the last of the bunch I nearly fainted of a heart attack. You see right there on top of the most gorgeous Red Delicious was the biggest and most grotesque spider I had ever laid eyes on, and I nearly touched on it with this here hand," she said wide-eyed as she held up both of her hands....one pointing at the other.

"Well, I jumped back so far and dropped the bag. All them apples go spilling right out all over the floor and down the aisles and ever which way and I just run! That's what I did I just run outta that there store and didn't stop till I got to the front door of my porch!" she said fanning her face with one hand.

"Next Sundee in church all these folks askin' why I's runnin' suh fast, and I tell 'em I thought I'd left the stove on! I's so embarrassed with myself, I lied!" she said with blushed cheeks.

I waited till the giggles from the jurors faded before I began.

"It's accurate that you were scared. Is that right, Laura?

"That's right... I ran cause I's scared silly!" said Laura giggling again with her hand slightly touching her lips.

"Thank you, Laura, that's all," I said.

I counted eight smiles from the jury as I made my way back to the table. Eight out of twelve.

"You may step down," said the Judge.

Prosecution called Mr. Rhodes to the stand. The courtroom was eerily silent as Rhodes made his way to the front of the courtroom. Rhodes appeared haggard and lethargic as he dragged himself onto the witness stand and sat down with a clumsy thud. We would need to go easy on him as the jury would be sympathetic to a parent who lost a child so brutally. After the swearing in, he lifted a glass of water to his lips with a shaky hand and drank the entire glass as the silent courtroom listened to each of five gulps. Rhodes set down the glass and cleared his throat.

Prosecutor Lipp approached the witness stand.

"Are you ready, Mr. Rhodes?" asked Lipp kindly.

"Yes, I'm ready."

The prosecutor stood near a jumbo size picture of Tessa. I remembered the photo from the Rutledge High Yearbook. The photograph took me instantly back to the first time I saw her and the impact she had on me. I never dreamed I'd be looking at it in a courtroom defending the boy accused of her murder.

"Mr. Rhodes, could you please describe for the jury your relationship with your daughter, Tessa?"

Rhodes looked at his own hands for what seemed like a full minute before he spoke.

"She... she was our life. She was everything to me and my wife."

His cracking voice and broken spirit broke our hearts and moved some of the jury instantly to tears.

"She was smart and good. She was the kind of kid that you marveled at. You wondered why the good Lord blessed you with such a beautiful child. She was kind and thoughtful. She cared about people... strangers too and she proved it by helping them. She tutored some of the poorer kids that were in single parent homes. All the kids in school... well they just loved her. They told me and my wife all the time how much they loved her. We're not the same people we were. Me and my wife, well we both died the day she left us," he said through hollow cheeks.

Sorrow filled the quiet room and several jurors dabbed at their eyes.

"Mr. Rhodes," Lipp began.

"Do you recall when you, your wife and Tessa used to walk by the Tennison Park Basketball courts on your way to Rutledge Academy?"

"Yes, I remember."

"Do you recall stopping to shoot baskets with the kids while Tessa and the players stood by?" said Lipp.

"Yes, I remember," he said with a fractured smile.

"What was that like?"

"Well, the kids were great. I'd stop and make a bet with them. If I could make at least one out of ten shots, I'd buy them all ice cream. Usually, I could make at least one."

The jury melted.

"We would all stand around and talk with our ice cream cones. Those are good memories," said Rhodes.

"Do you recognize someone in this courtroom as one of the boys from Tennison Park, Mr. Rhodes?" said Lipp.

"Yes, I do. That's him right there," he said pointing at Brandon.

Prosecutor Lipp moved closer to our table and Brandon hung his head.

"Do you recall, Mr. Rhodes, if you ever witnessed Brandon and Tessa converse?"

"Yes, they spoke. He give her a flower one time... a small rose. She put it in a glass next to the sink."

"Thank you, Mr. Rhodes."

"Your witness," said Lipp smugly.

It was my turn at bat, and I needed to tread carefully. Donny would keep his eyes fixed on the jury.

"Good afternoon, Mr. Rhodes," I said.

"Good afternoon."

"Mr. Rhodes, the boys at Tennison Park, would you describe them as mainly poor?"

"Yes, that's correct."

"And would you say that most all were from homes with limited means?" I said.

"Yes, I believe that all of them were poor."

"Mr. Rhodes, you spoke with a Detective Ray Combs throughout the investigation, is that correct?"

"Yes, that's right."

"You mentioned to the detective that your daughter, Tessa, regularly received anonymous bouquets of roses. Is that right?"

"Yes, that's right," said Rhodes.

"But there was never a signature on the card?" I asked.

"That's right, there was never a signature. I didn't think too much of it until she disappeared."

"How many bouquets would you say Tessa received, Mr. Rhodes?"

"Well, goodness, let me think here. There must have been at least a dozen or so that year," he said.

"Tessa received about a dozen arrangements – all of them contained a dozen red roses. Is that right?"

"Yes, that's correct."

"Mr. Rhodes, do you recall Tessa ever mentioning anything negative about any of the boys at Tennison Park Basketball Court?" I asked.

"No."

"Did Tessa ever say that any of the boys asked her out or wanted to date her?"

"No, I can't say that she did," said Rhodes.

I made my way over to the witness box to stand near Mr. Rhodes.

"Thank you, Mr. Rhodes."

"No more questions, your Honor."

"You may step down," said the Judge.

We were given a fifteen-minute recess which gave Brandon a chance to stretch his sore limbs. His battles at L.C.I. had resulted in permanent damage to his body. He was a young man with the gait of a seventy-five-year-old. I walked beside him at an unnaturally slow pace as we made our way outside the courthouse. Brandon smoked one Marlboro after another under the watchful eye of a C.P.D. officer while Brenner and I compared notes.

Before we knew it, we were summoned back into court. Again, I had to adjust my pace to align with Brandon's slow gait. I stayed close to him as we made our way through the crowded courtroom, his eyes darting back and forth across the room nervously. I put my hand on his arm and reminded him to keep his focus straight ahead.

"All rise," said the bailiff as Judge Phillips entered the courtroom.

"The court calls Donna Page to the stand," said the bailiff.

"Hi, Donna, how are you?" I asked.

"I'm just fine, thank you," she said with a warm smile.

"Donna, you were interviewed by Detective Ray Combs and in that interview, you mentioned a certain man that came into the shop periodically to buy roses," I said.

"Yes, that's right."

"You said he was "average" looking. Is that right?"

"Yes, that's right," she said.

"Was there anything besides his appearance or manner that you can recall that stood out?" I asked.

"Well, let's see. I do recall that he always seemed in a big hurry. Like he wanted to get out of the store just as quickly as he could," she said.

"Donna, you recalled one time that this customer, uh, "Mr. Average."

This drew a couple of giggles from the jurors, and I waited till the room quieted.

"You recalled that Mr. Average had an issue with his car once when he was at the shop, is that right?"

"Yes, that's right. He bought the roses, but then came back into the store to use the telephone. He couldn't get the car started and had to call for service," she said.

"You said the towing service was Buddy's Towing, is that right?"

"Yes, yes, that's right."

"And you also recalled, the very last time you saw this man was on the Fourth of July 1967, the same day that Tessa was killed, is that correct?" I asked.

"Yes, that's correct."

"What do you recall about that day, Donna?"

"Well, I was closed being a holiday and all. I heard a pounding on the door, and I ignored it and figured they'd see the closed sign, but they just kept on pounding. They wouldn't go away, so finally I went to the door, and I recognized him as having been in the store before, so I just let him in," she said.

"And what else do you recall, Donna, about that day?"

"Well, like I said, he was in a hurry to get in and out of there. He bought the usual dozen red roses and he paid in cash. He seemed particularly rushed on that day and more so when he had the car trouble."

"And you recall it was Buddy's Towing that serviced the vehicle?" I asked.

"Yes, it was Buddy's. I saw the tow truck with the sign on the side of the truck, so I know it was Buddy's," she said.

"How much on average does a dozen roses cost from Page's Floristry?"

"Oh, well, they go up a bit on Valentine's Day and well, Mother's Day, of course, but on average, the cost is right around $50 plus tax and well more if there's a delivery. So, that's roughly $60 per bunch with delivery."

"Sixty dollars, whew! That seems like an awful lot of money for someone of limited income to spend, now doesn't it?" I said.

"It would seem almost inconceivable to think that a person with limited means might purchase one bouquet, let alone one a month for a year, don't you think?" I asked.

"Well yes, I would agree. They're expensive, but worth every penny!"

Smiles from a few of the female jurors.

I handed a photograph of Kendall Morgan to Donna Page.

"Donna, do you recognize this man as the one who came into the store on occasion?"

"Yes, I do," she said.

"And this is the man who always paid in cash and is the same man who had car trouble on July 4, 1967?" I asked.

"Yes, that's right," she said.

I walked to the jurors and showed them the photograph of Kendall.

"Thank you, Donna, that's all."

Prosecutor Lipp made his way over to Donna with a sly smile.

"May I call you Donna?" said Lipp.

"Yes, you may."

"Donna, before the trial, you indicated that a man came into the store on several occasions and purchased a dozen red roses, paying only in cash?" asked Lipp.

"Yes, that's right, only in cash."

"Did you have any idea of the identity of the man?" he asked.

"No, none at all."

"And did you give him a receipt once or any time, that you can recall?"

"No, I don't believe I did. He was always in such a hurry," she said.

"So, you had no idea who he was, and he never asked for a receipt?"

"That's correct," she said.

"You indicated this man was white, approximately six feet tall, had no outstanding characteristics, and was generally, average looking?"

"Yes, that's right except I did notice that he had a ruddy complexion," she said.

"So how many men over the course of owning the shop would you say you've encountered with dark hair, average looks and let's say less than perfect skin?" asked Lipp.

"Well, I don't know."

"Maybe twenty, thirty, forty?" he asked.

"Well, having a business and all for twenty-five years, yes, perhaps that many," said Donna.

"So, it might be more difficult to identify someone with average features as opposed to someone with unique or more attractive features, is that right?"

"Well, I guess I would agree with that," she said.

"Very good."

"Thank you," said Lipp.

The court would reconvene on Monday morning, and we would call Kendall Morgan to the stand. Brandon's hand trembled as he reached for the handrail making our way down the steps of the courthouse. We prepped him for Monday's trial and then left him with a Charleston police officer who would escort him to the motel, one of several who would be stationed outside his room round the clock.

The phone rang just as Leah and I were putting Christopher to bed. She told me not to answer, but I didn't listen. It was Rudy, whom I'd been successfully avoiding for the past month. I got off the phone as fast as I could, but when I went back to the bedroom, Christopher was already asleep and Leah looked angry. I suddenly realized I hadn't been home early on a Friday night in a very long time.

"He wants me to meet him at his office in the morning. He has something important to tell me," I said.

"Tomorrow's Saturday," she said.

"I know. I'll see what he wants and get out of there as quick as I can."

Leah stopped what she was doing and gave me one of those looks. You know the kind. It's that blank stare that tells you nothing but everything all at once. Without a word, *the look* says, you're a dope and why are you even speaking? *The look* makes you feel as though you're back in third grade and you've accidently wet your pants while your classmates' snicker. *The look* steals all the confidence you've earned in your twenty-eight years and reduces you to nothing more than a tongue-tied idiot. I had never quite gotten used to it, but somehow over the past several months, *the look* had become a normal part of our routine.

I PARKED in front of Navy Park across from Rudy's office and watched a group of children dodging in and out of jets on a splash pad while their parents sat on benches. I was a half hour early, having stopped first at the motel to take breakfast to Brandon. Food, apparently, was something the '*Do Drop Inn*' didn't offer its guests. Rather than go inside, I decided to finish what was left of a strong coffee and slightly burned bagel. I wondered if Rudy might try and tag team with another partner to coax me into joining the firm. That, however, was a long shot and he knew it. Maybe he would try and dangle an attractive salary under my nose. Lord knows Leah and I could use the money. We were tired of the small apartment and having to scrape by to try and make ends meet. It sure would be nice to have a few extra bucks, buy a newer car and take a vacation in the summer. Nice thought, but we both knew working for Rudy would be a death march. I wasn't cut out to be a good old boy. Somehow within the Campbell gene pool, I ended up with majority of the moral chromosomes and that was fine by me. I had peace of mind, something money couldn't buy.

I noticed a black BMW parked two spaces ahead and watched as the owner quickly exited the building and made his way to the car. The man was tall, lean and well dressed. And one more thing – he looked awfully familiar. I strained to see against the glare of the sun on the windshield but caught a view of his face as he checked for oncoming traffic. He looked an awful lot like Robert Lipp, lead prosecutor in the Thompson case. What was *he* doing here?! My heart raced and I nearly choked on the coffee. Suddenly, I had the motivation I needed to go inside.

The receptionist hid her magazine when she saw me enter.

"Hello, you must be Des," she said looking me over with a flirtatious smile.

"Yes, that's right. I'm here to see Rudy."

"Yes, I know. Why don't you have a seat I'll let him know you're here," she said.

"Thanks, but I'll stand."

She picked up the phone and called somewhere upstairs while I hung around the reception desk working out my strategy.

"It'll be just a few minutes."

"That's a very nice outfit," I said.

"Why thank you!" she gushed, straightening her shoulders in a proud sideways pose.

"By the way, was that Robert Lipp leaving the building?" I asked.

"Oh well, I'm not. Well, I shouldn't really. Oh, well since you're Rudy's son, I can tell you," she said scanning the lobby cautiously.

"It was a top-secret meeting! No one was supposed to know he was here," she whispered with eyes as wide as China plates.

"They met in the Grand Conference Room! Just the two of them!" she said.

"No, kidding? The Grand Conference Room?" I said picturing myself accepting the Oscar for best actor.

Just then the phone rang.

"Front desk. Yes, ok."

"He's ready to see you now," she said.

"Thanks."

"It was nice to meet you," she said straining to watch me as I waited for the elevator.

"Remember," she said in a loud whisper holding one finger over her lips.

I gave her the *thumbs up* as the elevator doors closed in front of me.

Rudy's office was decked out the way one would expect from the head of a multimillion-dollar law firm.

Rich Mahogany wood panels lined the lower half of the room and colorful artwork was illuminated on walls. Two entire glass walls overlooked Navy Park and a bustling corner of historic Charleston. He was on the phone and motioned for me to sit down. I listened while he barked orders at someone on the other end of the phone.

"Get it done now and we can wrap this thing up," he commanded before slamming down the phone.

"How are you, son?"

"Fine, just fine," I said.

"How's my grandson?" he said with a two-second smile.

"Everyone's good, real good," I said hoping we could get to the point sooner than later.

"I have some information about the Thompson case," he blurted.

My stomach started to hurt as the bagel did somersaults in my gut.

"You see, lead prosecutor, Bobby Lipp is a buddy of mine. I ran into him just last week and he shed some light on the case."

I decided to hide the fact that I knew Lipp was here only moments ago.

"Oh?" I said.

"Well, it appears Brandon Thompson was more familiar with the Rhodes girl than anyone knew," he said.

"What do you mean?"

"Brandon had a sweater of Tessa's. It was found in his possession when he was arrested, but mistakenly never entered into evidence," he said.

"So, what does it mean?"

"We, well, Bob thinks he had a relationship with the girl, and she broke it off. That's why he killed her," he said.

"Can he prove it?" I asked.

"Brandon was seen leaving the Rhodes' home the morning she was killed," he said with fake solemnness.

"What!? Why wasn't this presented as evidence in the first trial?" I asked.

"A new witness has only now come forward," he said.

"His name is Levon Kotch and he's a neighbor of the Rhodes."

"How did Lipp find him?" I asked.

"I don't know, but he's willing to make a statement. Bob will let you know as soon as its ready," he said.

You mean as soon as he's paid, I surmised.

"You should consider dropping the case. The Thompson kid is guilty," he said matter of fact.

"Let the jury decide," I said while picturing my fist on his jaw.

"You should think about this more, Desmond," he said with more seriousness.

"I've thought about it. He's innocent. Stop wasting my time," I said making my way to the door and slamming it with a bang behind me.

Why didn't Brandon tell us about this!? I picked up Donny and we raced to the motel.

The officer in front of Brandon's room greeted us with a low grunt as he perused the morning paper.

We pounded on the door, but there was no answer. The officer grew nervous. He put down his paper and stood. We pounded several more times before hearing the click of a lock.

"Get dressed, we need to talk" Donny barked.

Brandon went into the bathroom and came out in gray sweatpants and an orange t-shirt with the letters L.C.I. across his chest.

"We received some information from the prosecution about you and Tessa Rhodes," Donny blurted.

"You were at her house the morning she was killed?" asked Donny.

Brandon said nothing.

"If you've lied to us, I'll drive you myself to L.C.I. right now!"

"No, please!" pleaded Brandon.

"Were you there?!" asked Donny.

Again, Brandon was silent.

Donny lunged at him, but I stopped him before he did any real damage.

"Stop! Wait…!" I shouted as someone pounded on the door.

Donny pushed me and released his grip on Brandon. He then moved to stand in front of the window to cool off.

I opened the door, and the officer pushed his way in.

"Everything ok?" he asked eying Brandon suspiciously.

"Yes, we're fine," I said.

Donny didn't say a word as he stared out the window.

We waited till the officer was out of the room and continued.

"This is your last chance. You either tell us what happened, or we walk," I said.

We waited.

Donny studied Brandon as we both prepared to leave. He sat on the bed, head down looking at his hands.

A minute passed.

I looked at Donny and with a nod of his head, we moved towards the door. We were almost to the elevator when the hotel room door opened.

"Wait!" shouted Brandon.

"Get back in your room," shouted the police officer.

Brandon wiped his face with a towel as we reentered the room.

"I was there, but I didn't kill her!" he cried.

"What the hell were you doing there and why didn't you tell us," Donny shouted.

"She… she left it at the basketball court," said Brandon.

"What, she left what?"

"The sweater. She left it and I brought it to her," he said.

"Did you talk to her?"

"No, she wasn't there. No one answered," said Brandon.

"What else?" asked Donny.

"Nothing," said Brandon.

"What?"

"What else are you holding back?" I asked.

"Nothing. That's it!" Brandon shouted through trembling lips.

Donny and I left the motel and drove in silence. We were both filled with doubt. Why didn't he tell us before? It didn't make any sense. We were his allies. Frustrated and angry, we went our separate ways. My mind raced. What if he didn't paint the mural on the boxcar on July 4? What if he lured Tessa to the tracks and she rejected him? I tossed and turned till nearly dawn.

It was raining hard on Monday morning, and I had overslept. It was 8:45am and I was due in court at nine. Why didn't she wake me? I jumped out of bed and ran toward the bathroom but not before something that looked like a yellow Lego dug hard into my right heel. Hopping to the sink, I splashed water on my face and grabbed the nearest comb. I was just about out the door when I saw it. A small piece of yellow lined paper neatly taped to the refrigerator door, and somehow, I just knew. I looked around the small apartment and felt the emptiness. She had taken Christopher and left me. The short note said she was tired of feeling alone. She needed to think about what she wanted and would call me later. I was sick to my stomach.

I walked into court late looking like I'd just showered in my clothes. Having stepped into a deep puddle, I was keenly aware of the squishing sound my water filled shoe made as I entered the packed room. Donny scolded me with his eyes, and we all stood as the judge entered the court-room.

Levon Kotch, took the stand first.

Levon, at seventy-six years old looked just shy of one hundred. He wore a scowl on his face, thick wire rim glasses and a heavy cardigan sweater even though the morning temperature was a balmy eighty-six degrees. Levon appeared old and worn out but determined. Again, we surmised he was paid handsomely and would sooner or later start spending his payoff. A little digging revealed Levon was waist deep in debt and had a bankruptcy to match. A retired mail carrier twice divorced. Hence the debt.

Prosecutor Lipp approached the witness stand and that's when Kotch smiled for the first time. Not just any smile, but a "thanks for the cash kind of smile."

"Mr. Kotch, how long have you lived in Charleston?"

"All my life at 233 Parker Lane," said Kotch.

"And is it true that you're a neighbor of the Rhodes?"

"Yep, I live two houses to the right…that is if you're coming from the left."

"Right," said Lipp.

"Uh no, I said left," Kotch corrected.

"Yes, I understand," said Lipp impatiently which garnered a few giggles from the jury.

"On the morning of July 4, 1967, you saw a young boy running scared from the Rhodes' home, is that right?"

"Objection."

"Sustained. Rephrase the question and be careful" warned the judge with tired eyes.

"On the morning of July 4, 1967, you saw a young boy running from the Rhodes' home?" asked Lipp.

"Yes, he cut across the lawn to the sidewalk and that's when I seen him!"

"What else did you witness, Mr. Kotch?" asked Lipp.

"I seen him carrying somethin', look like a sack."

"Approximately what time of the day was it when you saw the young boy, Mr. Kotch?"

"Well, I'd say it was about 10:30am cause that's when the paper supposed to be dropped and I was waitin' for it, but the dumbasses late, again," he said with a scowl.

"Mr. Kotch, please refrain from swearing in my courtroom," scolded the Judge.

Kotch apologized while Lipp gave him a dirty look.

"Approximately how many feet were you from the young boy when you saw him?" asked Lipp.

"I would guess about ten yards er so."

"Did you see his face, Mr. Kotch?

"It's him right there!" he said.

"Objection."

"Sustained. The court will ignore that last comment," said the Judge.

"Can you describe the young man that you saw, Mr. Kotch?"

"Yes sir, he's about 5'6", 130 pounds with light skin, sandy hair and carrying a sack.

"Did you recognize the young boy, Mr. Kotch?" asked Lipp.

"No, but he look jus' like that one there," he said pointing to Brandon. The reactions from three of the jurors, was obvious mistrust.

"Objection."

"Sustained. Strike the witness' answer and restate the question," said the Judge.

"Did you recognize the young boy, Mr. Kotch?" asked Lipp.

"No."

"Thank you, Mr. Kotch," said Lipp stone faced while trying his best to hide his annoyance at hiring this bone-headed witness.

"Your witness," he said.

Kotch was a lousy witness for the prosecution. This was going to be fun.

"Mr. Kotch, please state your age and address," I asked.

"I already told ya," he said.

"Answer the question, Mr. Kotch," barked the Judge.

"I'm 76 years old as of yesterday. I live at 233 Parker Lane."

"Thank you. Oh, and happy birthday," I said.

Smiles from the jury box.

"Mr. Kotch, what is your occupation?"

"Retired mail carrier, 40 years."

"Married?" I asked.

"No."

"Divorced?"

"Yes."

"Once?"

"Objection. Where is this going?" said Lipp.

"Is this going somewhere?" asked the Judge.

"Yes, your honor."

"Overruled." Wrap it up," he said.

"Once, Mr. Kotch?"

"Twice."

"Thank you," I said.

"It becomes a matter of public record when a person, any person, files for bankruptcy, Mr. Kotch."

"Have you ever filed for bankruptcy?" I asked.

"Objection."

"Overruled. This is going somewhere too?" asked the Judge.

"Yes, your honor," I said.

"Continue," said the judge with a sharp eye on Lipp.

"Have you ever filed for bankruptcy, Mr. Kotch?"

"No."

"No?" I asked.

"Well, yes," said Kotch.

"No, or yes?" I asked.

"Yes."

"Was it difficult to recall the bankruptcy, Mr. Kotch? I said.

"Yes."

"When did you file?"

Silence

"Answer the question," said the Judge, with mounting annoyance.

"Last year," he said.

"You filed last year but you couldn't remember?"

"Slipped my mind is all," said Kotch.

"Mr. Kotch your home is across the street and over two houses from the Rhodes home, is that correct?"

"Yes, that's right."

"Your honor may I show the jury?" I asked.

"Yes, you may."

I handed Mr. Kotch and the jury photographs of the Rhodes property in relationship to the Kotch property. The photograph clearly showed a wooded lot obstructing Kotch's view of the Rhodes' house.

"Mr. Kotch, is that your property on the top?" I asked.

"Yes, it is."

"And is this the Rhodes' home?"

"Yes."

"It looks to me there is a lot full of thick trees that block your view of the Rhodes' property," I said.

Silence

"How is it that you say you saw a young boy leaving the Rhodes' home when there isn't a clear view of the Rhodes' property?" I asked.

"And how is it you can recall the defendant leaving the property nearly five years ago and you can't even recall what happened in your own personal business last year?" I said sharply.

"It's 'cause me long-term memory is better than me short-term memory," he barked.

"Oh, I see. That's interesting. For most of us, it's the other way around," I said.

Giggles from a few of the jury.

"No more questions," I said.

The court adjourned for lunch, and we walked to a nearby diner. Brandon was quiet, but I sensed he had something he wanted to say. I scanned the room for a phonebooth and found one at the back of the restaurant. It was occupied by a young waitress lounging with both feet propped up against its wall, oblivious to my being there. I sat back down and avoided eye contact with Brandon while we waited for our order. Donny headed to the latrine. I wasn't hungry. All I could think about was Leah and Christopher and how miserable I felt.

Brandon cleared his throat before he spoke.

"I wanted to tell you," he said.

"You know she... she was the only one that was nice to me. She talked with me like I was somebody, like I mattered," he said looking down at the table.

"I would have done anything for her," he said.

"I went there only to bring her sweater," he said.

"I did like her. She's the only one that made me feel like a man," he said.

"But I never hurt her. Never," he said now looking directly into my eyes.

I knew what he meant. Tessa made me feel I mattered too, but still, there was a nagging doubt kicking around in my head and I couldn't think clearly. Leah had left me, and I was a basket case with little sympathy for anyone other than myself.

We finished lunch and headed back to court. You can tell a lot about how someone feels about you by how much they look at you. The jury watched us even when the prosecution was up to bat. They studied our interactions with Brandon. They studied Brandon. A few of them even smiled when I looked their way.

We questioned the boy from the stable, Billy Hamilton, who was now nearly twenty-two years old. He was a college athlete playing ball and studying business at Charleston Community College with a sparkling 4.0 average. He was polite, articulate and was blessed with good genes. Billy recalled every detail about that day in the stable on July 4, 1967.

I approached Billy sitting in the witness stand and thanked him for his time.

"Yes, sir, you're welcome," he said.

"Billy, you worked in the stable at Campbell Mansion from June of 1967 through August 1967, is that correct?" I asked.

"Yes, sir, that's right," he said.

"And you worked with a man by the name of Kendall Morgan, is that right?"

"Yes sir," he said.

"You recalled that on July 4, 1967, you observed Mr. Morgan leave the stable at approximately noon and return to the stable after 5pm, correct?"

"Yes, that's right. My shift ended at 5pm and I was sitting down to change shoes before leaving and that's when he walked right in front of me. Didn't see me sitting there," he said.

"Were you in the stable the entire day, Billy?" I asked.

"Yes sir."

"Was anyone else in the stable that day?"

"No sir. It was a holiday and most went into the village for the street parade. I was part-time help for the summer, so I worked on Saturdays."

"Billy, is there any chance Mr. Morgan could have come back to the stable without your seeing him?" I asked.

"No sir. I worked right up front near the door all day, so I could see through the open door and Mr. Morgan didn't return till 5pm. I could see where he parked his car from inside the stable," he said.

"Billy, can you describe Mr. Morgan when he walked into the stable that evening?"

"Yes sir. Mr. Morgan came in and walked real slow.... like he was in a trance. He was covered in sweat, and he had bloody scratches on his arms and face. I thought it was odd that someone would be scratched up from just driving in their car," he said.

"Did you speak with him, Billy?" I asked.

"No sir."

"Thank you, Billy."

"Your witness," I said.

Prosecutor Lipp approached the witness stand and propped one foot on the bottom ledge while he leaned in resting his arms on the railing. His intimidation tactic appeared to work. Billy shifted uncomfortably and jerked his head back when Lipp came in closer.

"Billy, what is it that you're studying in college?" asked Lipp.

"Business, your honor... I mean sir," said Billy.

"No, I'm not the judge, he is," he said sarcastically pointing at Judge Phillips.

"Oh yes, I'm sorry," said Billy.

Lipp smirked and the jury frowned. Idiot.

"Billy, what kinds of activities did you participate in during the summer when you weren't working?" he asked.

"Well, I would hang out with my friends."

"What did you do with your friends?" asked Lipp.

"Well, we would go to Scooters at night and play foosball. Things like that," he said.

"Scooters the bar?"

"Umm, yes, sir."

"Were you at Scooters on Friday night, July 3, 1967, Billy?" asked Lipp.

"Yes, we were there both Friday and Saturday nights."

"Did you drink alcohol on those nights, Billy?"

"Objection."

"Overruled. Get to the point," said the Judge.

"Well yes, we had a couple beers," said Billy.

"And what time would you say you left Scooters on Friday, July 3, 1967."

"Well, we close the place up usually," he said.

"Three, four am?" asked Lipp.

"Yes sir."

"So, you started your job at the stable at eight in the morning and got roughly five hours sleep, is that right?" asked Lipp.

"Yes sir."

"Let's confirm, that's not five hours of sober sleep, that's five hours of alcohol sleep," said Lipp.

"So, it's safe to say you were not in tip top shape when you arrived for work on Saturday morning."

"Well, I was a little tired."

"A little tired or a little hung over?" asked Lipp.

"Objection."

"Overruled."

"No further questions," said Lipp.

Judge Phillips, having a previous engagement, eagerly dismissed us just after 2:00pm. Two local police officers escorted Brandon back to the motel and Donny and I headed to the nearest pub. I gulped a tall Guinness and then quickly ordered another.

"Better slow it down, we have a big day tomorrow," said Donny as he thumbed through a small notepad.

"She's gone," I said.

"What?!"

"She took Christopher and the dog went to her aunt's in Mount Pleasant," I said.

"No wonder you look like crap."

"Said she's tired of being alone. I should have known."

Donny put his arm on my shoulder reassuring me the way he always did. He was a stubborn old man with a heart of gold and as we talked, I remembered why I had made the decision to work for him. Donny cared about people, but not just people he knew. He cared about everyone, even the throwaways, the ones no one wanted. He cared about the ones without parents and the ones with selfish parents. Donny looked at the heart of a person not what was on the outside and gave of himself effortlessly.

We paid the bartender and headed to the parking lot.

"We only have tomorrow. That's it. Get some rest. I need you, son, but Brandon, he needs you more," he said.

The apartment no longer felt like home. I couldn't wait till the trial was over so I could focus on fixing things with Leah, that is if she would ever talk to me again. I thought about Brandon some more and felt angry realizing I had lost someone I loved in exchange for someone I hardly knew and now didn't fully trust. I couldn't shake the fact that he lied about having been at the Rhodes' house. It ate at me nonstop and interrupted my sleep waking me nearly every night. Losing my family had my mind racing out of control, and I was an emotional wreck. Nothing made sense to me now and I wondered how I got myself into this mess. I heated yesterday's leftovers in a small saucepan and sat down at the kitchen table. I thumbed through a pile of mail that consisted of mostly bills and advertisements for things I couldn't afford. At the bottom of the pile was the picture we had pulled out of Brandon's cell. I studied the drawing of the tattoo on Kendall's arm and then flipped the paper to the other side. An abstract of bright color had been sketched using crayons, which was most likely the only art tool allowed at L.C.I. Unable to focus on anything outside of the courtroom, I was half paying attention, until I noticed a mark in the bottom right corner of the paper. It was so tiny and faded, I could barely see it. I stood and held it up under the light and read 'Brando' and that's when it dawned on me. Brando and Brandon were one in the same. Why hadn't I realized it before? Now it all made sense. Brandon was at the tracks painting the mural the day Tessa was killed just like he said. I saw the mural with my own eyes, remembering how massive it was and how it stunned me. I remembered Brando, the signature and the date, July 4, 1967. Brandon was telling the truth. He had been at the tracks painting the mural that day.

THE COURTHOUSE was packed. Groups of family members, reporters and witnesses watched us as we stood with Brandon waiting to go inside. An elderly woman with white-blue hair and a venomous glare never took her eyes off me. A Rhodes' grandmother on the father's side from the looks of her. I was nervous as hell and still angry at Brandon for not telling us everything. I said nothing since our altercation at the motel. He apologized, but it didn't matter. He withheld vital information. My marriage was in the toilet because of him, and I wasn't feeling especially friendly.

The bailiff opened the doors at 9:01am. Showtime. Our final chance to argue for Brandon Thompson's freedom had finally arrived. We had worked hard to get here, but at this point I couldn't care less. Exhausted and frustrated, all I wanted was to get this over with, try and pick up the pieces of my broken marriage and get on with my life.

I spotted Kendall Morgan. His chin hovered close to his chest while his dark eyes scanned the courtroom as though he were searching for someone. We knew Kendall was responsible for Tessa's death. The motive, however, was still unclear, but we surmised he killed her in a state of panic. All we knew for sure was that he bought the roses the morning of July 4th, 1967 and delivered them to Tessa. And we could prove it. Kendall had no alibi, and he was the last person to see her alive. We needed to break him.

Bailiff called Kendall Morgan to the stand at 9:15am. Kendall was a solid man. Although well into his fifties, his body was lean and hard. His arms were two large cylinders of solid muscle, and his thick legs pounded the floor as he made his way slowly up the aisle to the witness stand. He looked as though he had just come from the stable. His Carhartt's were dirt stained, frayed at the edges and torn open at both knees. Underneath the baggy overalls he wore a tattered white t-shirt revealing the faded tattoo on his right arm that Brandon had identified.

The room was silent except for the steady hum of heavy breathing coming from the witness stand. The jury watched Kendall closely as I made my way to the front of the room. It had been only weeks since I'd seen Kendall face to face. The dark circles under his eyes were more pronounced and the skin on his face drooped at the corners of his mouth. If he was nervous, he didn't show it. Naturally menacing in appearance, the jury studied him carefully.

"Good morning, Kendall," I said.

Kendall nodded but showed no emotion as I prepared to question him. His dark eyes followed me as I positioned myself between him and the jury.

"Kendall, you work at Campbell Mansion, is that correct?"

Silently he nodded.

"Answer the question please," said Judge Phillips.

"Yes."

"What kinds of things are you responsible for?" I asked.

"I do whatever he ask me to do."

"Can you give some examples of what he asks you to do?"

"I clean stalls, tend to horses, the grounds, things like that," he said.

"Errands, do you run errands too?" I asked.

"Yes, whatever he ask me to do."

"Who asks you to do things?" I asked.

"Rudy. Rudy Campbell."

"Do you ever question what Rudy asks you to do?"

"No, never. I do what he ask," he said.

"Were you working at Campbell Mansion on July 4, 1967?"

"Yes."

"Do you recall Rudy asking you to buy flowers and deliver them to a house on Parker Lane on July 4, 1967?"

Kendall was silent.

"Answer the question," said Judge Phillips impatiently.

"Don't remember," he said.

"Do you remember going to Page's Floristry on July 4, 1967?"

Kendall's face turned dark at the mention of Page's. He wiped his brow with a handkerchief and lowered his chin while his eyes fixated on mine.

"No," he said.

"Donna Page is the owner of Page's Floristry. She has identified you as a customer. Ms. Page also recalls a man matching your description purchasing roses on July 4, 1967."

"Objection."

"Overruled."

Lipp slammed a folder on the table which kept the judge's eyes on him for the remainder of the trial.

"Do you recall owning a 1959 Ford Galaxie, Mr. Morgan?"

"I don't know."

"Let me refresh your memory," I said.

"I have right here, a copy of a towing receipt for a 1959 Ford Galaxie signed by Mr. Kendall "Kit" Morgan which was repaired in front of Page's on July 4, 1967."

I walked to the witness stand and showed the receipt to Kendall.

"Mr. Morgan, can you please read the signature on the receipt."

"It's mine," he whispered.

"I'm sorry, can you please repeat that for the jury?" I asked.

"It's mine," he said loudly.

Kendall was beginning to get angry.

"Mr. Morgan, how many times did you purchase roses from Page's Floristry?"

"I don't know."

"But you did buy roses from Page's on several occasions, is that right?"

"Yes."

"Who asked you to do that?"

"He did," said Kendall.

"And who was that?"

"Rudy!"

"And what did you do with the flowers after you bought them?" I asked.

"I took them where he asked me to."

"Did you take them to Tessa Rhodes' house?"

"I don't know."

"You don't know?" I asked.

"I take them where he tell me to take them."

"Do you recall taking them to 235 Parker Lane on July 4, 1967 for Tessa Rhodes?" I said loudly.

Kendall's face turned to crimson.

"Answer the question," said the Judge.

"I take them where he asked me to!" he shouted.

"You took them to Tessa Rhodes' home on July 4, 1967. The same day she disappeared and was later found strangled in the woods near Tennison Park!" I shouted.

"Objection."

"Overruled," scolded the judge.

"What happened, Mr. Morgan, when you got to the Rhodes' house?"

Kendall began to breathe in loud gasps as I continued to grill him.

"I'll tell you what happened on July 4, 1967," I said.

"Kendall Morgan delivered a bouquet of roses to Tessa Rhodes. Normally, he would leave the vase on the front porch and disappear before anyone knew he was there. But this time.... this time, he was caught," I said directly to the jury. "Tessa Rhodes caught him! She threatened him, and that's when he panicked and struck her!" I said.

"No!" shouted Kendall.

"You put her in the trunk of your car and sped away from the house as fast as you could!" I barked.

"No!" he shouted, shaking his head fervently while sweat dripped from his face.

"Didn't care that a boy from Tennison Park was blamed for what you did! Didn't care that a young man spent four years behind bars getting the piss beat out of him every day of his life! Didn't care that a family was devastated by the loss of a beloved daughter and a community shattered by her death! Brandon Thompson didn't kill Tessa Rhodes. You did! I shouted into Kendall Morgan's face, so close I could see the pores on his skin.

"You took Tessa to the tracks and that's where you dumped her," I said as my hands trembled.

And that's when he broke.

His head fell into his chest, and he held his face in both hands and began to wail louder than I've ever heard a person cry.

"I'm sorry. I'm sorry. I didn't mean to. I didn't mean to do it," he sobbed.

His voice was muffled but loud enough for the jury to hear.

I walked over to the jury and showed them photographs of Kendall's tattooed arm along with a police report indicating Brandon's description of the man he saw at the tracks.

"Brandon Thompson heard Tessa's cry. He got scared and thought some-one was going to bust him for tagging, so he ran. He ran right into Kendall Morgan just ten feet from where Tessa's body was found. He ran all the way into Charleston and through the July 4th Street Parade. Brandon identified Kendall as the man with the tattoo on his right arm. The man in the woods at the tracks. That man, ladies and gentlemen is Kendall Morgan."

"That's all your honor," I said.

The courtroom erupted while the judge banged a gavel. Prosecution sat dumbfounded as Kendall Morgan was escorted from the courtroom by two Charleston Police Officers and Brandon Thompson smiled for the first time in four years. My hands were still trembling as I felt a light touch on my right shoulder and turned to see Mr. Rhodes. He looked into my eyes and nodded and then turned and left the courtroom. News of Brandon's exoneration spread like wildfire. Groups of reporters enveloped us as we made our way out of the courthouse, stopping briefly to give a statement to the press.

Twenty-four

It was after 9pm when I finally arrived home to the empty apartment. The trial ended in victory, but I had no one to celebrate with. I saw myself on the news and realized how much older I looked. The past two years had taken its toll and I was in rough shape. The dark circles had become a permanent part of my face and I noticed an unflattering bulge under my tie. I decided I needed to get some rest and much-needed exercise. I didn't know exactly when I would see Leah, but when I did, I wanted to look good. She avoided my calls which only made me more determined.

Brandon lived in a halfway house not far from my apartment. I would visit him regularly. He put on a few pounds and looked better than ever. He was making good progress. In the daytime he went to a trade school and in the evening, he would read, exercise and help with chores in a house he shared with four other men. Brandon was also enrolled in an art program a few nights a week and I got to see some of his work first-hand when I visited him at the art studio.

"You're really talented," I said, perusing a variety of canvasses.

Brandon smiled and cocked his head examining a painting he had just finished. He planned to hang the new one over the fireplace in the half-way house. Like the mural on the boxcar years ago, this one was equally good. I watched him as he sprayed in circular motions followed by splatters whipped from a small brush. The specs of paint landed on the canvass perfectly as if divinely directed.

"You should try it," he said, handing me a brush.

"What? No, I don't think I could do anything good with paint," I stammered.

Brandon set a medium size canvass on an easel and challenged me.

"Do it. Are you scared?" he asked with a playful smirk.

The lawyer in me couldn't or wouldn't turn down a challenge so I agreed. I felt silly standing there with a wet brush, but again he prodded.

"Just let it come from here," he said tapping his heart with his free hand.

I turned the easel at an angle to hide the hideousness I was about to produce.

Someone turned on a radio and we painted. An hour had passed and by the time I was done, I felt a calmness I hadn't felt in years. The mural I created wasn't half bad either. We cleaned up and walked down the empty sidewalk. Brandon and I got to know one another without the pressure of my representing him and we became friends. He talked me into joining him in the art studio on Thursday nights and the more I painted, the more I looked forward to it.

After weeks in the studio, Brandon and I had produced nearly 100 pieces we liked and wanted to show. We decided to hold an exhibit. We rented warehouse space in an eclectic neighborhood that bordered Tennison

Park. The space was cheap and big enough to showcase almost all the art. I bartered with a P.R. firm to get the word out and in exchange, I would help them with some legal filings and a rather complicated real estate transaction for one of the partners. More importantly, they liked the art which meant they would try harder.

Preparation for the exhibition took all my free time. Brandon and I spent the first two weekends cleaning out the place. The one level warehouse had brick walls and exposed pipes that dripped steadily producing several puddles of reddish-brown water. Rusted metal windows in the middle of twelve-foot-high walls would need some elbow grease if we wanted a cross breeze. The old warehouse was full of rusted barrels, old tires and debris. Mice scurried from every direction causing me to jump on more than one occasion. Brandon was unfazed. None of it bothered him having grown up in Tennison Park. Parts of the floor were cracked and lifted by tree roots encroached under the concrete, so we decided to stack the old tires on top of the cracks and use them as props for the smaller paintings. By the end of the week, we had filled nearly fourteen bags of trash. We had the place for only four weeks, so we had to work fast. We rented a pressure washer and spent a full day hosing down the walls and floor. After that, we lifted the overhead doors and let the place dry out while we sat on the old barrels drinking beer. It was nearly dusk, and we were covered in dirt but satisfied.

"So why did you do it," he said out of the blue.

"Do what?" I asked.

"Why'd you fight to get me out?"

"I don't know," I said.

"I wanted to do something worthwhile, I guess," I said while scratching at the label on my beer.

"I wanted to make my own decision about the kind of work I would do, and I wanted it to matter."

"But you're a rich kid. You could do anything you want," he said.

"I really liked art when I was a kid, but my parents would have none of that. They had me pegged as an attorney from the get-go," I said.

"I fought for you, but I was also fighting for myself. I'm free now too," I said.

The following weekend Brenner and one of the guys from the halfway house helped us with the electric which was in bad shape and probably dangerous. We were able to get four sockets to work and with a few extension cords, we could light the place up.

The P.R. firm was a good idea. They were well connected to the kind of folk that appreciated art and had the Benjamin's to pay for it. We had nearly seventy-five confirmed RSVP's including the wife of the mayor and the curator of a well-known art gallery near Battery Park. It was a good start and Brandon was thrilled. He was a different person outside of L.C.I. His family at the half-way house provided the structure and support he needed.

It was two hours before the exhibit and Brandon was nervous. He kept asking me how he looked, but I couldn't get my mind off Leah.

"Do I look good? I look GOOD" he said as he gazed into a full-length mirror and smoothed his hair with both hands.

"You look the same as you did yesterday," I said.

"No really, do you like it?" he said turning to me and stretching out his arms to show off a leather jacket with a diagonal zipper running the length of his torso. On the other half he wore purple Corduroy bellbottoms two inches longer than his legs.

"It's uh... artistic," I said trying my best to hold it together.

"You don't like it, but you don't know nothing except white shirts and suspenders," he mused, pulling one suspender and snapping it against my chest.

"Now that's what I call BORING!" said Brandon.

"'Boring? You're more colorful than the art," I said pushing his shoulder.

We play-boxed our way to the front entrance and waited for the guests to arrive.

The old warehouse was turned into something special. Spotlights hung from the ceiling illuminating the colorful tapestries. The overhead doors were opened all the way allowing a warm breeze to drift easily through the large space. We mingled through the crowd like a couple of amateur celebrities while soft jazz played. Soon enough nearly half of the artwork was sold. The remaining pieces would be on loan to two local galleries. I kept my eye on the entrance but there was no sign of her. It was almost 9:00pm and I was starting to get edgy. I couldn't keep my focus on any of the conversations and ended up excusing myself from several customers in mid-sentence. By 10:00pm I was angry, and I had had too many cocktails that looked and tasted like orange Creamsicles. I headed outside to get away from the crowd and Brenner followed.

"Look at him," said Brenner motioning toward Brandon.

"You did good Des," he said.

"I failed!"

"You saved someone," said Donny.

"But I lost someone too," I said as I hung my head and fought angry tears that started.

"You did the very best you could, and we won," he said.

"She left me!" I shouted.

By then some of the guests had made their way outside and hearing me shout, began to murmur.

"Hold on..." he said trying to calm me down.

"What good did it do me. I have nothing left!" I said as the cocktail glass shattered on brick.

"I don't feel like a hero right now. I don't care about Brandon Thompson. I don't care about the exhibit! I shouted.

"My life sucks!"

Brenner put his arm around my shoulder guiding me away from the crowd that had gathered. I pushed him away, but he stayed with me. He was smart enough to know when to be quiet and when to speak. He knew being without my family was killing me.

"Let's walk," he said.

We headed away from the warehouse and found an all-night coffee shop three blocks east. Brenner was a good listener and I needed him more than ever. We talked until after midnight, and by then I was sober, and we began to make our way back to the warehouse.

When we got there, most everyone had left including Brandon.

"What do you mean, where did he go?" I said to a thin weathered man from the half-way house.

"He took off down the street. Said you sorry for everything you did for him," he said.

"What!?" I shouted.

"He said you think he's not worth it," he said moving in close to my face provoking.

"I didn't mean that. Where is he?" I said.

"He gone, lawyer boy. He left that way," he said pointing toward Tennison Park.

"Close up for me, I'm going after him," I said to Brenner tossing him the keys to the warehouse.

I ran down Clark Street toward Main and headed East towards Tennison Park. After several blocks there was still no sign of him. Checking every open doorway and alley, he was nowhere to be found. Out of breath, I needed a break. I stopped and rested my back against a light pole in the heart of downtown Tennison Park. Frustrated and ashamed, I sat under the light holding my head in my hands not knowing where to go or what to do next. I had ruined the best night of his life.

I don't know how much time had passed before I heard it. It was faint at first but then the whistle grew louder. Finally, it dawned on me. I knew where he was. Brandon was where he always went when he was hurt. I was on my feet in an instant and ran as fast as my legs would go. I dodged across Water Street nearly missing a car that screeched its tires on the desolate street, its horn echoing through the neighborhood. I headed toward a row of broken buildings that bordered the tracks on either side. I jogged down the median stopping in each open car calling for him. I kept going deeper into the tracks and found myself in a familiar place. It was the section of the tracks I used to go to when I was a kid and wanted to get away from home. I had forgotten how peaceful it was and how much this place was a part of me. The moon over Tennison Park was bright and full. It lit the tracks and surrounding forest. There was still no sign of him, so I turned and headed back in the direction I had come from. I neared the caboose of a South Pacific line and saw a familiar tapestry on the side of a boxcar and a faint glow from inside. Someone was in the boxcar.

It was pitch black, but I knew he was there. I walked up to the doorway and rested one leg on the rusted ladder.

"I don't regret it," I said.

"All of it. I'd do it all again. Even losing Leah. I'd do it all over again," I cried.

"I can't let you believe that it didn't matter," I said stopping to wipe my eyes.

"You matter, Brandon! You saved me too."

"I'm an idiot and I'm sorry," I said.

A cigarette butt tossed from the boxcar landed at my feet, but he didn't say a word. After a minute I turned and began to make my way back to the exhibit. By the time I crossed Water Street, it was cold, and a light rain became a steady downpour.

I turned right onto Clark Street and that's when I saw them. A group of four Negros standing near Klein's Liquor in the alleyway. They watched me as I headed toward Main and that's when they began to follow me. I could handle myself with a couple of them, but not all four. I turned around and they were starting to close in. I kept a steady pace but when the street curved to the left, I was out of view and began to run as fast as I could.

They caught up with me in the center of a small playground and pushed me from behind. I hit the ground face first and then turned onto my back.

They were young, boys really, but they were big enough to hurt me. My only defense was to make some noise so I shouted as loud as I could. The biggest one came down hard and slammed his fist on my mouth. I struggled while the others held down my arms and legs. I was able to free one leg and kicked the little one in the mouth making him bleed. They began to punch and kick me while I yelled and struggled to get free. They yanked at my pockets and with each new kick kept asking, "where's it at?!" I was penniless so in their frustration, all they could do was kick me repeatedly and I curled up into a tight ball covering my face and head. They kept at it for several minutes till my arms were frail and no longer able to protect my head. I lay there on my side half unconscious for minutes.

Something drew their attention, and I was left alone on the wet grass. My head throbbed and every muscle in my body ached. I heard shuffling of feet and yelling. Barely able to breathe, I turned slowly and was able to open one eye, but all I saw were moving shadows. My mind wanted to run, but my body wouldn't allow it. My right hand felt broken, but I was able to wipe blood from one eye and that's when I saw him. Brandon was taking on three of them. The fourth one was gone. They came after him, but he was quick. He coldcocked one and then another. If anything at all, his years at L.C.I. had taught him how to fight and he was good at it. The last one made a run for it. Brandon started to give chase, but then he stopped and walked back to where I lay.

Twenty-five

A YOUNG NURSE CHECKED the I.V. attached to my right arm. The room was quiet except for a steady beep coming from somewhere behind me. My limbs ached and my whole body felt like it was encased in concrete.

"Good morning," she said with a smile.

My lips felt like two balloons. She followed my eyes that fixed on a container of juice, and she opened it.

"Here you go..." she said as she carefully placed the straw between my lips.

Her name tag said Angie and she was pretty and smelled nice. Honey blonde hair tied in a ponytail framed large brown eyes that were comforting to look at. Two dimples appeared on her face when she smiled, and her lips were covered in a shiny gloss with a fruity scent.

I was hoping I was in good enough shape to go to the bathroom on my own. I certainly didn't want a pretty nurse helping me do that. Brandon entered the room just as she was leaving. He stuck his head around the door to get a better look at her and then rebounded with a wide smile and a thumbs up.

"Don't even think about it," I mumbled.

"You look like dung," he said sliding a chair next to the bed.

"No kidding. What took you so long to rescue me?"

"I needed time to think about what you said.

I came to tell you. I forgive you," he said.

THE END

About the Author

The author lives on the shores of Lake Erie in beautiful Buffalo, NY. She is an unapologetic believer in the impossible.